The wedding mar~~ch~~ unseen hands ope~~ned~~ from the inside. K~~ate began her~~ procession down the aisle and Helena's heart started to pound.

Even though it was silly—it wasn't ever going to be a real marriage—nerves dotted her skin with pinpricks. Helena locked her gaze firmly on the bouquet in her hand, which was why she didn't see the way that Kate stiffened and almost missed a step.

Helena didn't, in fact, see much until she was nearly halfway up the aisle because it was only when Kate stepped to the side, glancing in panic between her and the man at the top of the aisle, that Helena realized that something was wrong.

Something was terribly, horribly wrong.

Because standing at the top of the aisle, the six-foot four-inch dark-haired, bronzed Adonis wasn't the man who had promised that he'd do everything in his power to help her. No.

Standing at the top of the aisle was the last man she'd ever expected to see.

Leonidas Liassidis.

The Greek Groom Swap

One wedding, two billionaire brothers...but who will be getting married?

A marriage of pure convenience? Check.

Vows simply to secure an inheritance? Check.

Amicable divorce scheduled in advance? Double check.

Correct groom waiting at the altar? *No!*

What do you do when your oldest friend agrees to be your temporary husband, then swaps places with his estranged twin brother on the day of the wedding? CEO Helena Haddon must say "I do" anyway! Then she'll send her maid of honor, Kate Hawkins, to retrieve the runaway groom before scandal ensues...

Find out what happens to Kate and Leander in

The Forbidden Greek by Michelle Smart

And dive into Helena and Leonidas's story

Greek's Temporary "I Do" by Pippa Roscoe

Both available now!

Greek's Temporary "I Do"

PIPPA ROSCOE

HARLEQUIN® PRESENTS™

Recycling programs for this product may not exist in your area.

ISBN-13: 978-1-335-59360-3

Greek's Temporary "I Do"

Copyright © 2024 by Pippa Roscoe

For questions and comments about the quality of this book, please contact us at CustomerService@Harlequin.com.

TM and ® are trademarks of Harlequin Enterprises ULC.

Harlequin Enterprises ULC
22 Adelaide St. West, 41st Floor
Toronto, Ontario M5H 4E3, Canada
www.Harlequin.com

Printed in Lithuania

MIX
Paper | Supporting responsible forestry
FSC® C021394

Pippa Roscoe lives in Norfolk near her family and makes daily promises to herself that this is the day she'll leave the computer to take a long walk in the countryside. She can't remember a time when she wasn't dreaming about handsome heroes and innocent heroines. Totally her mother's fault, of course—she gave Pippa her first romance to read at the age of seven! She is inconceivably happy that she gets to share those daydreams with you all. Follow her on Twitter, @pipparoscoe.

Books by Pippa Roscoe

Harlequin Presents

The Wife the Spaniard Never Forgot
His Jet-Set Nights with the Innocent
In Bed with Her Billionaire Bodyguard
Twin Consequences of That Night

A Billion-Dollar Revenge

Expecting Her Enemy's Heir

The Royals of Svardia

Snowbound with His Forbidden Princess
Stolen from Her Royal Wedding
Claimed to Save His Crown

Visit the Author Profile page
at Harlequin.com for more titles.

For Amy Andrews,

Not only an amazing author, a wonderful woman but also an incredible friend.

Thank you so much for sharing your beautiful home with me.

xx

PROLOGUE

Eleven years ago...

HELENA WIPED HER damp palm on the silky material of the black dress her best friend had picked out especially for this moment. She wanted it to be just right, which was why she and Kate had talked about it non-stop since Helena had got back to boarding school in September from the summer holidays.

Spending Christmas on the Liassidis private island, just off the coast of Greece, was the best present her parents could have given her. Getting to see Leo and Leander in between the summers she and her parents spent here in Greece? A Christmas miracle!

Helena checked herself in the reflection of the mirror in the hallway outside Leo's bedroom. She'd put her hair up in a fancy bun and even made an effort with her make-up. Her mother had raised a critical eyebrow and deemed it unsuitable with a single word that had cut like a knife. But her father had patted her on the shoulder and told her she looked beautiful—*'very grown-up'*—salving the dull ache her mother had caused.

But that was what she'd wanted, right? To look grown-up. She was fifteen now, not the little kid that Leander and Leo always joked about her being. She pressed her lips together. She knew why she didn't want them, want *Leo*, to see her as a 'little kid'. And she wasn't stupid either. She knew he had a girlfriend, that he would never be interested in her in that way. But there it was…that little candleflame flicker of hope that wouldn't quit, no matter what she told herself.

Her fingers clenched reflexively and accidentally crinkled the carefully wrapped present she'd spent ages choosing and personalising. She pressed a hand to her chest to soothe the funny, turning twist it did at the thought of giving it to Leo, reminding herself to breathe.

She looked up and saw the boughs of rich green foliage Cora had decorated the house with just for her. Helena knew that in Greece they didn't traditionally decorate their homes with holly and mistletoe in the same way that they did in the UK, but that Mrs Liassidis had done that—for her—touched her deeply. Helena *loved* the Liassidis house with its incredible view over the Aegean that she couldn't get enough of.

But really, the best thing about it was Leonidas and Leander. The twin brothers might have been six years older than her, but they made her feel like family. Leander made her laugh and laugh and laugh, but Leo…

'Helena, really. Isn't it time for you to stop being so foolish? Leo's six years older than you.'

Helena felt a painful blush rise to her cheeks. Despite her mother's words, she wasn't actually stupid enough to think that she'd marry him like her father and Uncle Giorgos joked about. Giorgos Liassidis wasn't really her uncle but her dad's business partner. Only he felt like an uncle and Helena loved the way he was with his wife, Cora, the easy affection between them. And she liked how her parents were when they were here. Because when they were back in England she didn't really see much of them.

Helena shook off the thought and focused instead on the Christmas present she'd bought Leo. It was completely different to the one that she'd bought Leander, which she knew he'd like, but...the one for Leo was different. It *meant* something.

He'd been so different since arguing with Leander a few years back and starting work at Liassidis Shipping. She'd wanted to make him *happy* and had thought that her present for him might at least make him smile again.

She got to the landing outside his room, her heart pounding in her chest and her palms a little damp again. *Nervous.* Why was she nervous? She smiled at herself for being silly and went to knock on the door, but...

'It's fine, I don't know what you're worrying about,' she heard Leo say in a tone Helena didn't recognise. It was joking...but patient?

'I just want to make a good impression.'

Helena scowled at the whining tone she recognised.

'Mina, you've met them loads of times before.'

'But this is different. It's *Christmas.*'

Helena leaned closer to the door and realised that it was open a sliver. Her heart shuddered as she saw Leo pull his girlfriend into his arms and she willed back the hurt. She was being stupid again. Of course, Leo would be with his girlfriend.

'I suppose that *she'll* be here. Helena.'

For the first time, Helena almost regretted learning Greek. A part of her wished she couldn't understand the conversation, but she couldn't make herself turn around and leave either. The bitterness that Mina had spoken with had cut Helena. But not as deeply as realising that Leo didn't come to her defence.

'Of course she'll be here. My father invited her parents.'

'She's such a brat.'

'Mina, she's harmless.'

Helena's throat was thick with hurt and her cheeks hot from a painful flush.

Harmless.

'I've seen the way she looks at you. That's not harmless. I know, I was that age once.'

The present crumpled in her hands as Helena clutched it tighter, shame burning into her skin.

'She follows Leander and me around like a puppy,' Leo dismissed.

'Then train her better,' Mina's voice snapped out.

'Mina, she's just a child.'

'Trust me, that's something you have to nip in the bud. And it's really unfair of you to lead her on.'

'Lead her on?' Leo asked, the confusion in his tone clear. 'Mina, I think you've misunderstood. She's nothing to me. Just the daughter of my father's business partner. That's all.'

Unable to see past the tears in her eyes, Helena spun away from the door and down the corridor. She pulled up short at the top of the stairs.

She's just a child. She's nothing to me.

She clenched her jaw so hard her teeth started to ache, and furiously wiped at the tears in her eyes. How could her heart hurt and pound so much at the same time? She took a shuddering breath but it did nothing to ease the pressure in her chest. Another tear fell down her cheek and she wondered why it felt as if a rope tying her to shore had been cut. As if she were a boat drifting out to a stormy sea without an anchor.

She looked down at the present in her hands, the box slightly crumpled, and knew she couldn't give it to Leo. Not now. Humiliation crept across Helena's skin and settled into her stomach.

She thought of the cubbyhole that Leander, she and Leo sometimes used to leave silly notes or treats for each other. It was hidden behind a small painting just down the hall. With a numbness creeping over her, she went to the painting and shoved the present into the hiding cubbyhole, hoping that no one would find it for a very long time.

Her throat thick with hurt, she forged that feeling into resolve. Mina had nothing to worry about. Helena wouldn't look, or think twice, about Leonidas Liassidis ever again.

But as she wiped her eyes and made her way downstairs she didn't see Leander step out from the shadows, concern and sadness flicking between Helena and the door to his brother's room. He shook his head, before slowly following Helena down to where the rest of their families were gathered.

CHAPTER ONE

'TELL ME AGAIN that I'm doing the right thing.'

'You are doing what you *need* to do.'

'Am I?'

'Helena, if you want me to talk you out of this, I can… I don't care about the guests, the church, the press interest all of this hoo-ha has gained, or the damn money.'

'Hoo-ha?'

'Yes, Helena. Your wedding is a load of hoo-ha,' Kate said with such seriousness, Helena didn't know whether to laugh or cry.

Groaning, she turned away from her reflection in the mirror. 'You're right. It is a load of hoo-ha. Just think what would happen if they all knew the truth,' Helena said as her heart lurched guiltily.

That this marriage was a farce, a sham, utterly fake. But it was also the only way to fix the terrible situation she was in—the only way to save her charity, Incendia.

'If only they hadn't been whipped into a frenzy by *Leander the Lothario*,' Kate joked.

Helena smiled at Kate's teasing. Leander Liassidis might have been the eternal playboy cruising through life like he didn't have a care in the world, but for Helena, when she needed it, he'd been her rock and her saviour. She loved Leander like a brother and the only thing that ever caused her any worry was the hope that one day he might find someone that he could love sincerely. Which was perhaps a tad ironic, considering that in less than twenty minutes Helena would be walking down the aisle to stand beside him in front of one hundred and fifty guests, where a priest would declare them husband and wife.

'If only my inheritance didn't have the most ridiculous strings attached to it,' Helena wished out loud.

'What on earth was your father thinking?' Kate demanded. 'As if access to your inheritance should ever have depended on a man.'

Helena's heart turned as it always did when she thought about her father. He had passed away just after her sixteenth birthday and not a single day had gone by that she hadn't thought of him, hadn't missed him.

'To be fair, if I could have waited just two years until I was twenty-eight, none of this would have even been necessary,' Helena countered.

'Of course. Also, perfectly reasonable,' Kate said sarcastically. 'A woman matures only when she marries a man or when she's nearly thirty!' she cried.

Helena couldn't help but smile. Their unwavering defence of each other was what made them strong, their bond closer than family because it had been chosen. And Helena would choose Kate every single day.

'I'm sure my mother would have helped me fight it, if there had been time,' she insisted, missing the sceptical look that passed across Kate's features. 'But challenging a will in the courts would take too long and draw too much attention. The financial review of Incendia is due in December. The police have advised that they won't have caught Gregory by then, and even if they do, they won't be able to return the money he stole until after a full investigation and a lengthy court case,' Helena said, shaking her head.

Helena had never believed that she'd one day get to work at the charity that had been a lifesaver to her when she'd needed it. After the loss of her father, her abrupt return to boarding school had been hard. Her fear of falling asleep and never waking up—just like her father had done one awful June night—was at risk of becoming full blown and permanent insomnia. So her tutor had recommended Incendia to her. There she'd received grief counselling and support while she underwent the genetic testing to see if she had inherited Brugada syndrome, the disease that had killed her father.

While the test had eventually come back negative, it was with Incendia that she'd got to see first-hand how much good that charities could do, how integral they were to providing support for people in need. It had inspired her so much that she'd changed her study direction immediately to focus on attaining a business degree at Cambridge, swiftly followed by her master's in Non-Profit Management.

Her mother thought that she was being foolish, throwing away financial security for misplaced altruism, but Helena had found her passion, and not only that, something she was good at.

Her first job had been with a small charity start-up and she'd relished the opportunity to throw everything she had at it. It paid off and she soon became known for having a head for business, and a fresh, exciting approach to gaining partnerships that were relevant and contemporary to younger generations. Connecting people who were sincere about helping, rather than seeking out borrowed kudos, was what made her unique. Her hard work made her peerless.

And then six months ago it had happened; Incendia had asked if she might be interested in a role as their CEO. It had been the most amazing moment of her life. She had celebrated with Kate and even Leander had made a special trip to London to take her out and treat her to a congratulatory meal that had ended up—as it usually did—with him seeing her safely home in a taxi, before he escorted whatever woman had taken his fancy back to his London apartment.

But within a month following her start at Incendia, the CFO had quit and disappeared with nearly one hundred million pounds in investment funds. Shocked and horrified, she'd gone immediately to both the police and the charity commission. She'd spent days locked in meetings with Incendia's trustees, where she discovered that the previous CEO had failed to renew the business insurance that would have made this painful rather than disastrous.

Because if there wasn't a way to cover the shortfall in money, Incendia wouldn't survive long enough to see what the police could recover. A financial review at the end of the year would declare them bankrupt and all of the people they could help, all of the families Incendia supported, the research into medical conditions that affected millions around the world...would be left with nothing.

Helena *couldn't* let that happen. Incendia had been there for her when no one else had been. She'd *needed* to find a way to fill the hole made by the missing money and there was only one way she could think of.

The shares her father had left her in Liassidis Shipping.

Staring at her reflection in the mirror, she felt that sense of loss keenly. The shares were the last piece of her father that she had left, and she'd never wanted to part with them. She'd hoped to leave them in the business now run almost completely by Leonidas Liassidis, simply content for that to be her connection to the company her father had founded with Giorgos Liassidis. That was all she'd wanted. To know that her father's legacy lived on. To know that a part of it still belonged to her. But now she would have to let them go. Let *him* go.

A little piece of Helena's heart broke under the weight of the sob she kept locked in her chest.

She felt two slender arms come gently around her shoulders and looked to the mirror to meet Kate's eyes in the reflection.

'It's the right thing to do,' Helena said, unsure who she was trying to convince more, herself or Kate. It was what her *father* would have done, Helena was sure of it. 'I can sell the shares as soon as the marriage is registered in the UK and there will be enough there to cover the shortfall in Incendia's accounts.'

'Do you think you could buy back the shares, once you have what you need?' Kate asked gently.

Helena bit her lip and looked down at her feet. 'No.' She wouldn't lie to herself about this. She couldn't afford to. 'Only a fool would sell shares in Liassidis Shipping,' she explained. Only a fool or someone extremely desperate. And she was extremely desperate.

'Well, then,' Kate said in her no-nonsense way. 'We have a plan, we're going to stick to it and we're going to get it done!'

Helena smiled at her best friend. 'I really like that colour on you,' she said, glad that she had chosen gold for her only bridesmaid; Kate looked absolutely radiant.

Kate smiled, shrugging a delicate shoulder to the mirror and pouted. *'Merci!'*

There was a knock on the door and Helena turned, hoping that it might be her mother, but it was just the officiant letting them know they were ready.

Helena turned back, masking the hurt before Kate could see it. Yes, it was foolish to hope, and she probably should have known better after all these years, but she felt peculiarly alone standing in the small church library that had been given for her to get ready in on her wedding day, without either of her parents there with her.

Pushing that thought aside, she looked at herself in the floor-length mirror.

The deceptively simple wedding dress suited her slim figure. She'd been teased as a teenager for resembling a kitchen towel tube and had never really liked her lack of curves, but the dress by a new Spanish designer—Gabriella Casas—made her look and feel beautiful. A puff of laughter left her lips at the irony. It would be utterly wasted on

Leander Liassidis, who had never looked at her as anything other than a little sister.

As Kate told the officiant that they would be right there, Helena touched the silver bracelet her father had given her on her sixteenth birthday. It was the last present he had given her, barely weeks before he'd passed. She was both sad and relieved that he was not here today. Sad because even though this wasn't ever going to be a real marriage, the small child in her still wanted her father here on her wedding day. But she was also relieved, because he didn't have to see what she was about to do. Shame stung her skin as she fought an internal battle of wills. She wanted to be a businesswoman that he could have grown to respect, that he could be proud of. And she could still do that. But only if Incendia survived.

'Are you ready?' Kate asked from behind her.

Helena nodded.

It was a short walk between the church library and the entrance to the rather grand chamber of the Catholic church in Athens. Helena might have wanted to have a small ceremony with very little grandeur, but Leander had his way in the end.

'It's going to be my only wedding—we might as well make it a party!' he'd exclaimed.

She just hadn't realised that Leander's 'party' would attract so much attention and so much 'hoo-ha', as Kate had said earlier.

If she was honest, she'd been utterly thrown by the press interest in them. Yes, the Hadden name had notoriety in the UK, but in Greece, the Liassidis name was on a whole different level. The press had been stalking them ever since the news became public, each subsequent headline more hysterical than the previous one, the whole of Greece and beyond taken by the friends to lovers fairy tale.

Anyone who was anybody was there, wanting desperately to be seen. In truth, Helena had only cared about a handful of people. Her, Kate, Leander, obviously, and his parents, Giorgos and Cora. She wasn't naïve enough to think that his twin brother would come. Leander and Leo hadn't shared a single word in the last five years. Her heart pulsed once. She hadn't spoken to Leo since the bitter confrontation he'd had with her mother nearly ten years ago, after Gwen had naïvely thought she could continue her father's work with Liassidis Shipping.

She would be there in the church, with her second husband John, who had reluctantly agreed to interrupt his golfing holiday, and Helena tried to tell herself that it was enough that they had come.

She and Kate paused outside the large doors that would open to the nave of the church, listening for a moment to the gentle hum of conversation and the soft sounds of string music. Helena wasn't religious, but she couldn't help but wonder if it was sacrilegious to marry in this way, in this place, for reasons that had nothing to do with love.

'We could run, you know. I've got the car keys,' Kate whispered as if sensing her hesitation.

Helena laughed and turned to see Kate's reassuring smile, the easy confidence she had radiating over Helena like a balm.

'No. I'm good. But thanks though,' Helena said.

'Loves ya,' Kate said, causing Helena to grin at the favourite phrase passed back and forth between them.

'Loves ya,' Helena replied. 'Now, let's do this.'

The wedding march started up and unseen hands opened the doors from the inside. Kate began her procession down the aisle and Helena's heart started to pound. Even though it was silly, it wasn't ever going to be a real marriage, nerves dotted her skin with pinpricks. Helena locked her gaze firmly on the bouquet in her hand, which was why she didn't see the way that Kate stiffened and almost missed a step.

Helena didn't, in fact, see much until she was nearly halfway up the aisle because it was only when Kate stepped to the side, glancing in panic between her and the man at the top of the aisle, that Helena realised that something was wrong.

Something was terribly, horribly wrong.

Because standing at the top of the aisle, the six-foot-four-inch dark-haired, bronzed Adonis wasn't the man who had promised that he'd do everything in his power to help her. No.

Standing at the top of the aisle was the last man she'd ever expected to see.

Leonidas Liassidis.

Leo stared at the closed doors of the church, silently cursing his arrogant, reckless brother to hell and back, utterly uncaring that he did so in a church.

He was furious. How *dared* Leander do something like this?

If Leo hadn't picked up the message his brother had left him little less than three hours ago, he wouldn't have even been here. As it was, he'd barely made it on time.

Leo cursed silently again.

He hadn't spoken to Leander in five years and *this* was the first thing his brother had asked of him?

'Be me.'

There had been more on the message, but now as he stood at the top of a church aisle in front of one hundred and fifty guests, it was all Leo heard.

'Be me, be me, be me.'

They hadn't pulled this stunt since they were boys. Back when he'd still considered Leander his brother, before his lies had betrayed the future that Leo had thought he would have with Leander by his side. The future Leo had wanted.

Time hadn't dulled the memory of the day they had turned eighteen, when their father had offered them a choice: inherit Liassidis Shipping, beginning a three-year handover period from him to them, or take a sizeable fortune and strike out on their own.

They'd spent *years* of their teenage lives talking about what they would do with Liassidis Shipping. Years, planning how to make it the industry number one, how they would rule together, side by side, sharing all decisions and doing it all together.

And right up until that moment, Leo would have sworn he knew his brother better than he knew himself. But when their father made the offer that had been made to him by *his* father, Leo had looked at Leander and seen a stranger staring back at him.

Even the thought of it rippled tension across the muscles of his back. Betrayal, fury, a potent phosphoric taste in his mouth. Leo clenched his teeth together, painfully aware that he was the sole focus of the entire congregation at that moment in time. And in that congregation were his parents, staring at him, looking horrified.

Because although he and Leander were truly identical—to the point where the number of people that could tell them apart could be counted on one hand—his parents had recognised him the moment he had entered the church.

But he had been ushered immediately up to the top of the aisle before he could tell them what was going on. And even if he *had* been able to speak to them, what would he have said? Would he have repeated what his brother had said when he'd left his message?

That Leander had 'needed time'?

Time for what, the *maláka* had not even bothered to explain.

Leander had insisted that he would be back by the end of the honeymoon, but Leo didn't believe him for one second.

Helena needs this. Really needs it. So please. I'll ask...beg. But please, don't leave her alone on the wedding day.

Leo clenched his teeth again, a thin lightning strike of tension spreading up his neck and jaw. Of all the women in the world, his brother had chosen to marry Helena Hadden? Leo would have been happy to have lived the rest of his life never seeing or hearing of a Hadden woman ever again.

There had been a time when things had been different. When he'd enjoyed Helena's company, when he had almost thought them friends. But that was before Helena had taken Leander's side following his betrayal, and things had only become worse three years later, after what her mother, Gwen, had done to Liassidis Shipping following the death of her husband.

Whether it had been grief or sheer stupidity, Gwen's actions had nearly destroyed Liassidis Shipping for ever by engaging the competitor of an existing client at a knockdown price. It had taken everything, *everything*, Leo had had in him, to pull it back from the brink of ignominy.

Christós, what was he even doing here?

He looked back at the church doors. No matter how much he resented the Haddens, and hated his brother, he couldn't have left Helena alone to face down a near obscene number of wedding guests, let alone the press corps camped outside. No, only his selfish, uncaring brother would do such a thing. And he—Leo assured himself with an almost violent intensity—was *nothing* like his brother.

The sound of the doors opening screeched against the floor, causing him to wince momentarily at the shocking intrusive sound. And then, just for a second, he saw her centred in the doorframe, smiling at her bridesmaid, her face filled with hope and excitement, and it cut through the red haze of his anger.

That wasn't Helena Hadden, his body roared.

The effect she had on him was instantaneous, his stomach tensing against a punch to the gut, as heat worked its way around his system. The woman standing in the ivory sheath was statuesque tall, beyond beautiful, and barely reminiscent of the gangly girl he'd last seen ten years before. The sheer marked difference between what he saw and what he'd been expecting destroyed any instinctive barrier against seeing the intense feminine beauty of the woman standing at the opposite end of the aisle and he was frankly relieved when the bridesmaid came to take her place in front of the bride.

Get yourself together. Right now.

Reminding himself who she was, what her mother had done—what his brother had got him into—tuned his feelings back to where they should be. Right around the time that the bridesmaid stepped aside and Helena caught sight of him.

He was staring at her so intently he saw the exact moment she realised it was him standing at the top of the aisle, not his brother. Shock and horror morphed quickly into anger, the fire in Helena's startling blue eyes burning him as badly as that first impression of her had.

And yet he could do nothing—say nothing—until she reached his side. And even then? They were facing the entire congregation and because *someone*—probably his egotistical brother—had the genius idea to have the priest stand with the congregation rather than with them, as tradition would dictate, they were in full view of absolutely everyone.

Helena needs this. Really needs it.

Leo bit back a scornful laugh. One look at the sheer panic in her eyes was enough to tell him what he needed to know.

This was no love marriage. Not that he'd have believed it even if they'd tried to deceive him. There had been absolutely no trace of such feeling between her and Leander in all the years that the Haddens had spent with his family. So Leo could be forgiven for thinking that it was a joke when the wedding invitation had first arrived. He'd left the thick embossed cream paper on the corner of his desk, almost needing to see it again and again just to believe it.

That was until the press and the gossip magazines had started to whisper rumours that 'Leander the Lothario' was finally settling down.

What had started as a few pieces in lifestyle magazines had taken Greece by storm. The Liassidis family name combined with, Leo would grudgingly admit, Leander's own achievements were lauded throughout the country. It should have come as little surprise that this mockery of a love story would have captured the nation's attention.

But Leo had seen members of the international press right by the steps of the church. Was that why his brother had decided to cut and run? Or was there another reason? Did it even matter, Leo asked himself, as his brother had once again proved that only his own needs and desires mattered, uncaring of who he hurt in the process?

He turned his attention back to Helena, who was mere steps away, and she was *still* glaring at him with a fury that promised nothing less than hellfire.

Finally, she stepped up beside him, her eyes locked onto his face as if *he* were the one who had put them in this situation, rather than his brother. As if he didn't have better things to do with his time than to play groom in whatever scheme Helena and his brother had cooked up.

She pasted a smile over exquisite features and hissed out from between her teeth, 'What are you doing here?'

'Your beloved fiancé has done a runner,' he returned with an equally false smile and gritted teeth, aware that the gaze of every person in the room was on them. If he hadn't been the employer of nearly twenty thousand staff around the globe, he might have found the experience a bit intimidating.

He looked back at Helena to see that the blood had drained from her creamy complexion.

Malákas.

This time, he wasn't sure whether he was cursing his brother or himself.

'He said he'll return before the end of the honeymoon,' his hitherto unknown conscience prompted him to add.

In her wide eyes he could see her thoughts churning like a sea swell in the Aegean, but they were just as unfathomable to him.

'Smile,' he warned as he registered a ripple of unease pass across the guests in the church.

She flashed another glare at him that didn't need translating. It was the eye-squint equivalent of *Don't tell me to smile, damn you*. But she did exactly as he'd said. She turned to face not only the priest but also the guests, the delicate rosebud of her lips widening. And Leo could have sworn he heard a collective sigh pass across them as if she'd bestowed them with a gift.

The priest welcomed the guests in English and began

the wedding service, but he could have sworn that he felt Helena's panic tugging at his senses, inflaming his own frustration that his brother had involved him in such a scheme.

And as the choir began the first of what he hoped was only a few carefully selected hymns, Leo only had one thing on his mind—getting out of this ridiculous situation as quickly as possible—which was why he went through the process of saying what was needed to be said, when it needed to be said.

Honeymoon be damned, the moment this ceremony was over he was done. Out. Back to his apartment in Athens, back to Liassidis Shipping, where several important meetings and events would consume his thoughts. Not the quagmire of chaos that surrounded both Helena and Leander.

The priest gestured for them to enter the vestry, where they would sign the marriage document, and if anyone thought it odd that Leander Liassidis had grasped the hand of his soon-to-be wife and rushed her away from the view of the congregation it was only put down to just how passionately he loved the beautiful Helena Hadden.

CHAPTER TWO

'DON'T TOUCH ME,' Helena commanded in a harsh whisper, painfully conscious of the guests not terribly far away, her head swimming and panic crawling across her skin.

'I'm not,' Leo growled, his hand hovering near the base of her spine having the same impact as a red-hot poker would have. He turned back to the priest and his parents, following just behind.

'*Parakaló*, Father, Mamá, Patéra…would you give us a few minutes? We would like to just take in this beautiful moment.'

This beautiful moment?

Leo's words tripped around her head and she thought it half a miracle that they couldn't hear the insincerity dripping off them like poison.

Cora glanced between them and Helena nodded to let her know that it was okay. Helena hadn't seen as much of Leander's parents as she would have liked since the showdown between Leo and her mother following the mistake Gwen had made with Liassidis Shipping, and Cora's concern touched her deeply. But if Helena had even a single hope of figuring out what was going on,

and how she was going to fix it, she would have to talk to Leo. Right now.

She watched the priest and Leo's parents leave the small, ornately decorated room. Turning away from the powerful impact his mere presence had on her, she was confronted with the cloth-covered table—a large book open to display the marriage schedule detailed in beautiful calligraphy. And there, mocking her, were empty spaces waiting for their signatures. No, not theirs, *his*.

Leander's.

Without that, she would never be able to access the shares that she needed to save the charity.

Oh, God, what was she going to do?

She spun back to face Leo, taking a step closer than she had intended, her worry, her concern so strong.

'Where is he?' she demanded, unable to keep the panic from her voice.

'How should I know?' demanded Leo, as if affronted she would even ask that of him.

He peered down at her, apparently uncaring of how close they were standing. And she hated the way her body responded, as if he were the man of her dreams instead of her nightmares. They were almost chest to chest, pressed against the superfine of the dark impeccable wool of his three-piece suit, the pristine white shirt that smelt of cotton and sandalwood, and she fought the temptation to inhale deeply. Because if she did breathe in, her chest would push against his and—

Leo stepped back so suddenly she nearly stumbled forward. Humiliation coursed through her as she regained her equilibrium, turning away from him to take that much needed breath.

'There must be some mistake,' she insisted.

'The only mistake you made, *agápi mou*, is trusting Leander for even a single second.'

'Don't call me that,' she lashed out, resenting the affectionate moniker that had no place between them.

She leaned back against the table and looked resentfully at the man who was seemingly unaware that he was standing in a sunbeam that picked lovingly over such incredibly handsome features. Helena knew that most people had a hard time telling the Liassidis twins apart, but she had never fallen foul of mistaking one for the other.

It was as if she could sense their personalities as much as what they looked like. Leander was playful, fun, irrepressible to the point of distraction. The week that she, Kate and Leander had just spent together in the lead-up to the wedding had been full of parties and fun, drinking and dancing. They'd been staying at the private island owned by the Liassidis family while his parents were away and she'd sensed absolutely nothing wrong with Leander. No, as always, he'd been his larger than life, gregarious self.

But if Leander was the life of the party, then Leo was the hangover in character form. The painful reminder of the morning-after, of earthly responsibilities and recriminations—that mistakes must be punished and paid for.

And while their features were near perfect symmetry— the thick, raven-dark hair almost wilfully unruly, the patrician nose, the savage cut of cheekbones regularly wept over by models, the closely cut beard that looked insolently stylish and the broad determined forehead—there *was* a difference.

Leo had always held himself back. He was just that little bit more isolated, that little bit less gregarious than Leander, a trait that had only increased with time and their separation, as if their differences had become more marked.

Because Leander had *never* impacted her the way Leo did—like her breath had been stolen, like flames heated her skin, like her pulse, her body even, was attached to the snap of his fingers, ready to leap at his whim.

Helena cleared her throat, suddenly painfully aware that she had been staring at him.

'What did he say to you?' she asked.

'Here. You can listen for yourself.'

Leo pulled his phone out of the pocket of his trousers and pressed the screen. Within seconds, Leander's voice filled the small room.

'It's me. I know we've not spoken for...well. You know how long it's been. I need you to do something for me. I have to go away. I just need some time... I'll be back by the end of the honeymoon, but until then I need you to do something for me. I need you to be me. I know you're not going to want to. But Helena needs this...'

Leo pressed a button on the screen, stopping his brother's message.

Helena frowned. 'Is that all there is to the message?'

'All that's pertinent to this situation,' he replied, not

entirely sure why he had cut off the message there. But he knew instinctively that she wouldn't have wanted to hear Leander beg him not to leave her alone on her wedding day. Not because she wouldn't appreciate Leander's concern, but because he, Leo, had heard it.

She was staring at his phone as if there was more. As if there was some kind of explanation still to come.

'He wouldn't do this to me,' she said, lost in her thoughts. 'He knows…'

'He knows what, Helena? Why you're performing this absolute scam of a marriage?' Leo asked, refusing to disguise the scorn and disdain he felt for her and his brother in that moment. He hated lies, detested dishonesty, and it didn't get much more dishonest than this. 'What is it? What could you possibly hope to get from this?' he demanded, finally at the end of his patience.

Helena bit her lip. He could see the struggle in her eyes. Azure blue, misting over with sea spray.

'The *why* isn't pertinent to the situation,' she had the audacity to throw back at him.

'Fine. It doesn't matter anyway. The moment that the priest comes back, I'll tell him I'm not signing it and I'm done. Out,' he said, cutting through the air with his hand.

The effect on Helena was instantaneous, as if she'd been burned by fire. She launched herself across the vestry, her hands in little fists, raised as if she was holding herself back from actually clutching onto the lapels of his suit jacket.

'Please, Leonidas, please. I… You can't,' she said hopelessly. 'I… I need you.'

The words seemed to shock them both.

'Then tell me what this is all about,' he demanded.

She nodded fast, and a thin tendril of wheat-blonde hair unwound from the chignon. Helena began to pace and he began to feel uneasy for the first time that day.

'Helena—'

'I'm thinking!' she exclaimed. 'I'm…trying to figure out where to start.'

She turned on him mid-stride.

'Do you remember the shares my father left me?' she asked, her eyes bright shards of blue piercing him straight in the chest.

Of course he remembered the shares her father had left her in Liassidis Shipping. They tormented him each shareholder meeting where decisions were made that determined the future success of his company.

After Leander had taken his father's money and disappeared, Gwen Hadden's ignorant and stubborn decision had nearly destroyed the company, and it was Leo—alone—who had poured blood, sweat and tears into returning Liassidis Shipping to its rightful place as the number one company in the global industry. He had worked furious hours, with no one and nothing to guide him but his grit, instinct and determination. And he alone was responsible for the outcome.

In the years since he had fully taken over from his father, Leo had built up a global client list, with even more desperate to work with him. But the knowledge that anyone, let alone a Hadden, would one day inherit the thirty percent of Liassidis Shipping shares that her father had left her in his will had *tortured* him. He hated that, like her mother, Helena could impact the company's decision-making process. He hated that he didn't have complete control over a company that should be entirely his.

'*Naí*, of course I do, Helena,' he bit out.

She pulled her top lip beneath her teeth. 'The terms of my father's will state that I will inherit those shares—'

'When you are twenty-eight years old. Yes, I know. Two years' time.' The date had been indelibly printed on his brain ever since he'd heard the terms of the will. It had been like a bomb, ticking down until the day he no longer had a decent grasp on his company.

'Do you remember the caveat?'

Leo frowned. 'No, I... What caveat?' he asked, his stomach beginning to shift uneasily.

Helena swallowed. 'I can inherit those shares earlier than my twenty-eighth birthday if I marry.'

Leo felt as if he'd been slapped. Shock poured into every cell of his being.

'Why do you need the shares, Helena? What are you going to do with them?' he asked, realising suddenly that, no matter what played out here today, no matter where his brother was, whether he came back at the end of the honeymoon or not, his own life was about to change irrevocably.

Helena squared lean shoulders and faced up to him.

'I'm going to sell them,' she declared mutinously. 'As is my right.'

Helena had heard the phrase *a face like thunder*, but never actually seen it until now.

'You're going to sell the shares,' Leo repeated, almost

word for word, as if making absolutely sure that he'd heard her right. 'Do you have *any* idea how that could impact Liassidis Shipping?' he demanded hotly. 'Any at all? How could you be so—'

'Keep your voice down,' Helena hissed.

He inhaled an angry breath and turned around, but Helena didn't miss the way that his fists clenched as if he'd hoped they were wrapped around her neck, before he plunged them into his trouser pockets.

She watched the shift of the wool suit jacket over the shoulders he rolled and as he cricked his neck from one side to the other. He stood so tall within the vestry, he nearly took up all the space.

'Who?' he asked, without bothering to turn and look at her.

'Who what?' she responded, not quite sure what he meant.

His exasperated sigh echoed around the room. 'Who are you selling the shares to?'

Helena frowned. To be honest, she hadn't thought that far ahead. She didn't need her business degree, or her master's, to know that the moment she had access to the shares there would be a feeding frenzy. People would bite her hands off for Liassidis Shipping shares.

She should have been pleased, but she wasn't. The thought of selling the shares her father had left her in a company he and Giorgos had built from the ground up devastated her. It was her father's legacy—the only thing of his that she had left, after her mother had sold the house and everything in it while she'd been away in her last year at boarding school, 'desperate to move

on with my life,' she'd explained in the phone call that
had taken away the last of what had once been Helena's
entire life.

'You haven't decided yet,' he accurately guessed,
pulling her back into the present.

The hairs on the back of her neck rose in warning.
She could see the wheels turning behind Leo's fierce
eyes. The intensity in them was as hypnotic as it was
unbearable and she had just realised what he was about
to say when the words came out of his mouth.

'Sell them to me.'

'No.'

Leo laughed, cruelty masked by remarkable beauty.
'It's not as if you're in a position to refuse me.'

'What are you going to do?' she demanded. 'Marry
me? It's Leander's name on the register, not yours,' Helena pointed out.

'And the only people that know I'm not my brother
are you and my parents. And it's in none of our interests to reveal the kind of fraudulent activity we're about
to embark on.'

'You're mad. Crazy. You would never put Liassidis
Shipping in such a risky position. What if we were discovered?' she demanded.

'The reward is worth it.'

*To have you removed from anywhere near my com-
pany*, she all but heard him add in the silence.

An ache bloomed deep within her heart from one
too many rejections but she told herself it didn't matter.

'And you're desperate,' he pressed. 'I don't need to
know what you need the money for, whether you spent

too much on pretty clothes, or whether Gwen has tried to destroy another company,' he dismissed, uncaring of the effect his words had on her. 'All that's important is that you need to sell the shares, and I am in the position to buy them the quickest. So, tell me what you need in exchange for them.'

And at that moment she truly hated Leonidas Liassidis. Of all the things he'd ever said about her, of all the things he'd done after her mother had made an easy mistake for someone utterly new to business, *this* was what Helena would resent him for the most.

Making her feel weak and vulnerable, *to him*.

'It's not just the wedding,' she finally admitted through gritted teeth. 'It needs to be unquestionably a marriage. Leander...before he left, arranged for us to attend events throughout the next week—'

'The honeymoon?'

'Yes. We're supposed to attend various events to be seen, to prove that this is a real marriage. So that when I register the marriage certificate in the UK there are no questions then about me accessing my inheritance.'

'You need me to pretend to be him.'

'I need you,' Helena grudgingly explained, 'to pretend to be the affectionate, playboy, charming husband that Leander would have been.'

'I can do that.'

'You have as much charm as a venomous snake,' she hissed. And while everything feminine in her roiled at pretending that Leonidas Liassidis was her 'loving husband', she couldn't deny that he could give her what she needed quickly and without fanfare.

'How much?' she asked, cutting to the heart of the matter. She thought she saw a flash of surprise, but it was gone in the blink of an eye.

'Fifty million. For *all* your shares.'

Helena nearly choked. 'That's nearly a third of their market value, Leo. That's daylight robbery,' she accused, horrified. She'd expected to make nearly two hundred million from the sale.

He shrugged as if to say *take it or leave it*.

'Absolutely not!' she cried out angrily as pinpricks of sweat dotted the back of her neck.

It wasn't enough. Not nearly enough to replace the money stolen from Incendia.

'Okay,' Leo said amicably. 'It's your call. I'll just slip out the back and you can explain to all the guests that my brother has disappeared to leave you stranded and alone on your wedding day. I'm sure that the press will have more sympathy for you than him. But, to be honest, none of this will affect me in the slightest.'

He turned and before she could stop herself she'd reached out to grab his arm. He paused, looking down at where her hand had grasped onto his sleeve as if he couldn't believe she'd dared.

She removed her hand and he turned slowly to give her his full attention. How could she have ever thought there was anything remotely decent about this man? It had been years since they had properly spoken, more years before that since they had laughed together. Just the thought of it seemed nearly impossible. And now? She couldn't ever imagine laughing with this man again.

He was blackmailing her with an offer that was so offensive it made her feel nauseous. But what choice did she have? If she didn't agree to his offer, then there was no way that she could hope to plug the shortfall caused by the CFO's theft. And if she didn't, then the charity would be declared bankrupt by the financial review in December. Millions of people, families experiencing loss and devastated by cardiac events, would suffer. All because she hadn't been able to fix it.

'I don't need to know what you need the money for... All that's important is that you need to sell the shares, and I am in the position to buy them the quickest.'

Leo was right in one way. But he had also made a big mistake in revealing how much he wanted to have the shares for himself. It was a weapon. Small, and not enough to beat him, but enough to get what she needed.

'One,' she threw out between them.

'One what?'

'One hundred million.'

His head snapped back as if he'd hardly expected her to even think, let alone dare, to actually counter his offer.

'No.' The word was a full stop cutting through the air.

'Okay,' Helena said, putting her hands on her hips. 'You're right. I'll call this off. I'll figure out a different way to solve my issues. And I'll *still* have thirty percent shares in Liassidis Shipping,' she taunted.

Tension snapped across those broad shoulders, making him appear to loom more imposingly over her. He went very still, as if fearful that if he moved the wrong way he might lose the one thing he most wanted. Those shares.

'And then, when I'm twenty-eight, just think of what I could—'

'Seventy-five.'

'No.'

Leo slammed his teeth together before he could say another word. Helena Hadden had learned how to negotiate. There had been a time when her face had been so expressive that he could have sworn he'd all but seen her words before she said them, but now? Staring back at him was a fury who had chosen the hill she would die on. He couldn't afford to underestimate her like he had with her mother, or this time the damage could be fatal.

And really, if he was honest, offering fifty million for thirty percent shares in Liassidis Shipping was almost disgusting. One hundred was still nauseating. But it was a drop in the ocean of what Gwen had cost the company, so Leo told himself that the deeply unfair price was nothing but compensation years after the event.

He could have let her sweat a little more, but they didn't have time. He could feel the restlessness of the guests waiting in the nave, the concern building between the priest and his parents.

'One hundred.'

She held out her hand as if to seal the deal.

'I'll have my people email you the contract,' he said, ignoring her hand and turning back to call for the priest, missing the way that Helena masked the jagged edge of pain that crossed her features.

His parents, thankfully, remained studiously quiet while the priest went through the legal requirements.

Helena was first to sign the register, her gaze flicking to his one final time before the pen flew over the dots beside her printed name.

Unaccountably, his pulse picked up. Looking down at the piece of paper, the jarring sight of Helena's name beside that of his brother tightened a grip around his chest. Recognising it as a reasonable response to the chaos his brother and Helena were dragging him into, he placed his pen on the paper.

Signing this was the height of stupidity. If they were ever discovered, it would absolutely destroy his reputation and in all likelihood be the very end of the company— and after he'd worked so hard to bring it back after near bankruptcy.

But if they *weren't* discovered then he would finally have the whole of the company to himself. Without another thought, Leonidas Liassidis signed the register as his brother.

Five minutes later, he took his place beside Helena in front of the priest and the wedding guests and counted down the minutes until he could get away from the church and Helena and get a drink in his hand. The reception would at least afford him some space from her, he prayed, as the priest's words washed over him. Until…

'In the sight of God and these witnesses, I now pronounce you husband and wife! You may now kiss!'

His mind went utterly blank for a moment, the pulse of blood rushing in his ears became thunderous, even as he leashed himself back under control. He turned to face Helena, studying her carefully, her eyes wide with shock and something close to fear, but not quite. He half-expected her to run, but she didn't. She simply watched him, her gaze a physical touch against his senses.

He raised his hand to the side of her face as if to cup her jaw, but stopped short of touching, and he chose to ignore the ripple of response across Helena's features, chose to ignore his body's instinctive response to her as a woman. Because his brain had absolutely no trouble remembering just how far he needed to keep from Helena Hadden.

She watched, wide-eyed, as he dipped his head. He felt the entire congregation in the church hold their breath in anticipation, surprised to realise that Helena had done the same—the blue depths of her eyes beginning to disappear beneath the black of her pupils.

Leashing an instinctive response, he dipped his head deeper, cutting off the line of sight to their lips from the guests in the church, and lowered his thumb to Helena's mouth. He slid the pad of his finger across the slick surface, blurring the gloss coating of the flushed plump lips, trying to ignore the subtle flinch that pulled at Helena's body as he did so.

Oohs and *ahhs* filled the nave of the church and the only person who would ever know that they hadn't kissed was his fake bride.

CHAPTER THREE

'WHAT THE HELL is going on? Where is Leander?' Kate demanded as she drew a still reeling Helena away from the reception. The loud voices of guests could still be heard at a painful volume to Helena's sensitive ears. But the small cloakroom was thankfully quiet and empty of guests, who were being distracted with canapés and chilled glasses of champagne.

She felt… She shook her head, still trying to rid herself of the humiliation that had stung her cheeks irrevocably with shame. She had *wanted* Leo to kiss her. With an old familiar need that had filled her senses and overwhelmed all rational thought, she had wanted him to kiss her and, as if unable to bear even the smallest of touches, he'd only made it *look* like he'd kissed his bride.

'Helena? Are you okay?' Kate tried again, pulling Helena around to face her. 'You're beginning to worry me.'

Helena was worried too. She pressed her fingers to her lips, hoping to feel something other than Leo's thumbprint there. A shudder rippled through her. Disgust, she told herself. Anger.

'Helena!' Kate cried, finally pulling her back to her senses.

'I'm sorry,' she said. 'I'm… Leander's gone,' she admitted helplessly, without realising that Kate had somehow recognised that the man standing at the top of the aisle had been the wrong Liassidis.

'I know that. But where?' she demanded.

'That's what I'd like to know,' Leo said, standing across the threshold as if as reluctant to enter as she was to have him there. As it was, he filled the doorframe of the small cloakroom, stifling the air and making Helena feel claustrophobic.

Kate glared at him. 'Actually, that's not important right now. Are you okay?' Kate demanded of Helena.

Being cut off by a complete stranger, being told that what he said wasn't important, left an almost comical look of shock across Leo's features and Helena enjoyed every single moment of it. Bastard. It was the least he deserved.

'Yes, I'm okay,' she told Kate. 'I don't know where Leander is, but Leo is going to stand in for him while he's away.'

'Away? This isn't making any sense, Helena.' Kate's pretty features scrunched in confusion.

'He just said that something came up and that he'd be back by the end of the honeymoon,' Helena explained.

'That's it? He didn't say anything else to you?'

'It wasn't said to Helena, it was left on my—'

'Well, we have to find him,' Kate announced, cutting off Leo once again.

Leo's response was a glare that would have felled many a man, but Helena's best friend couldn't care less.

'Do you know where he'd go?' Kate asked Helena.

'Why would she know where—' Leo tried before Helena cut him off this time.

'He could be anywhere, but I'd imagine he's in one of his properties. He's probably thinking that there are too many for us to check them all. But I need him. He needs to be here,' Helena said desperately.

'I'll find him, Helena. I promise,' Kate swore, the look in her eyes telling Helena that Kate knew how much this meant to her. So much was on the line—and just because Leo had promised to cover for his twin didn't mean that he'd actually be able to pull this off. If people found out—the press even—it would be a nightmare of unholy proportions.

'My jet will be at your disposal,' Leo informed them.

Kate looked at him blankly. 'Is that supposed to impress me?'

Leo glared at her. 'I don't like you,' he said boldly.

'That's okay, I don't like you either,' Kate replied, turning back to Helena. 'If you can give me a list of his properties, I'll take the jet and find him. I'll go now.'

'No. Not yet. You're supposed to be giving a toast. If you disappear it would look like something's wrong,' Helena said, thinking through the rest of the reception. All she had to do was get through the next few hours and then, when she got to the villa on the Mani Peninsula that Leander had booked for their honeymoon, she could breathe, think and plan.

She had this. She would get through this and get what

she needed, because she was a Hadden. She was her father's daughter and people counted on her. Incendia counted on her. She wouldn't let them down.

Kate nodded in understanding. 'What about after the toasts?' she offered and Helena agreed.

Helena desperately didn't want Kate to go. As the only person who knew the whole truth about why she needed the money, who knew how much it had hurt to discover that someone had abused the charity that had meant so much to her in such a way, who had taken advantage of her new appointment to do so, Kate being away at a time that she most needed her would be terrible.

'Just think of it as practice for Borneo,' Kate replied, alluding to the fact that her best friend was finally achieving her dreams, having secured a permanent position as a vet at an orangutan sanctuary in the Southeast Asia island. Just the thought of her friend being so far away caused a pang of hurt to unfurl within her. But she pushed it aside. Kate had wanted this for so long.

'Okay, but if you don't find him in three days, that's it. You've got too much to do before Borneo and I can't let you mess it up.'

Kate gave her the dazzling smile that soothed her more than Helena could say. 'It's all done! I'm ready. Packed and everything. And don't worry. I'll probably find him hiding out at the first place I look.'

Leo had taken out his phone and was typing away. Both of the women looked at him expectantly—and when he looked up, he simply stared back at them blankly.

'Do I have permission to speak now?' he asked drily.

'Don't sulk,' Kate replied. 'It will give you wrinkles.'

Leo's eyes flashed, but Helena cut off whatever he was about to say with a question.

'Is the jet nearby?'

'Yes,' he replied, frustration clearly still simmering in his gaze. He turned to Kate, handing her a card, both reluctantly and resentfully. 'Give this to the pilot and crew. They'll help you with whatever you need, they'll take you wherever you need to go. Just…be nice, okay?'

Kate flashed him a sugary smile. 'I *am* nice,' she replied sincerely. 'To those who deserve it,' she said, before slipping out of the cloakroom and back to the reception.

Helena didn't bother hiding the smirk on her lips. It was nice to see someone put Leonidas Liassidis in his place for once. Especially as she couldn't do it herself. No matter what she felt towards the man, she needed him. At least until Leander returned.

'What did you tell her about me?' Leo demanded.

'Nothing but the truth,' Helena replied tartly, before slipping past him to follow Kate back to the reception.

Leo was getting a headache. Sitting at the head of the top table next to Helena, the sunlight bouncing off starched white linen, glistening glass and pristine silverware combined with the noise from the guests made him grimace.

'Could you at least try to smile?' Helena whispered angrily.

'It's a little hard to find something to smile about at this present moment,' he whispered back.

'Just think of all those shares you're getting at a bargain price,' Helena hissed through gritted teeth and, much to his surprise, he did actually smile. Something that seemed only to anger Helena more. So much so he could have sworn he heard a growl coming from her, which in turn only made him smile more and her scowl.

Looking out across the room, he could have counted the number of people he recognised on one hand. He had become such a stranger in his twin brother's life that the only people he knew were the bride and his own parents. Not that he cared. If these people valued his brother in spite of his selfishness and his ability to betray in a heartbeat, then more fool them.

Because wasn't this the ultimate betrayal? Not even turning up to his own wedding.

A wedding Leander had agreed to only to help Helena access her inheritance.

He was stopped from following that chain of thought by the way that Helena was craning her head to search the room.

'Is something wrong?' he asked.

'No, I just…' Her voice trailed off when her eyes settled and a small hopeful smile crossed her features. Her hand rose in a half wave, as if unsure how it would be received, and when he turned to look he found Gwen, acknowledging her daughter with a barely cracked smile.

He watched, leashing an old familiar anger as Gwen leaned to say something to her companion—her second husband, he presumed, the one she'd married about a year after her debacle with Liassidis Shipping. The man—John, if he remembered rightly—was something in banking.

As she came to greet her daughter, Leo was struck by the impression of seeing Helena in thirty years' time. Blonde hair adeptly highlighted with elegant silver streaks. High cheekbones and a strong jawline that had resisted age's pull. Gwen Hadden was slightly smaller than Helena, who had inherited her height from her father, but the poise was inherent to both women.

'Darling,' Gwen said levelly. 'The dress looks beautiful,' she went on with no tone of warmth in her voice at all, 'despite being from such a relatively new designer.'

Helena gazed carefully back at her mother, as if waiting.

'But really, having Kate dressed in gold,' Gwen added. Leo was surprised to feel the scold in her words. And Helena, who had been so fiery, who had been so full of life demanding he increase his offer for her shares, biting back a hurt Gwen *must* have been able to see.

'I'm so pleased that you and John could make it,' Helena said with a sincerity that seemed wasted on the woman.

Leo looked back to where John remained at the table, still eating his starter and engaged in conversation with another guest.

'Well, it did interrupt his golfing holiday, but he'll make up the time later. Will we be seeing you at drinks in October?'

Helena blinked. 'I'm not quite sure yet—the end of the year is a busy time at work.'

'Well, it would be good to see you there,' Gwen said before turning her attention onto him.

'Leander,' Gwen finally acknowledged.

Helena placed her hand on his, and to the world it would look like the affectionate connection between a newly married couple. Obviously, they couldn't see the crescent moons digging into his palms from her nails. He managed to keep the smile on his face despite the scratch of pain.

He nodded in return, suddenly unwilling to risk opening his mouth.

Gwen turned back to Helena one last time and Leo thought he saw the shadow of emotion flicker in her gaze.

'Your father...' She stopped, pressing her mouth into a firm line before pushing on. 'He would have been happy today,' she said, nodding to herself as if she had done some great maternal duty.

And, for just a moment, the years dropped away, the arguments, the feuds, the recriminations, and Helena was a little girl again, looking for her parents' approval. He saw it in the sheen across her eyes.

It was enough, Helena told herself through the dull ache that edged her breathing. It was more than she'd expected, she reasoned, and then told herself off for being silly. She had to remind herself that this wasn't a real wedding. It shouldn't mean anything to her that her father *had* joked about joining the families together. And she shouldn't be wishing for more than her mother was capable of giving.

Helena watched Gwen return to her table before daring to cast a look at Leo, whose expression was unfathomable. It was, she realised, the first time he'd seen her mother since the argument between them that had resulted in Gwen quitting and selling her Liassidis Shipping shares back to the company.

He reached for his wine glass and took a healthy mouthful as she remembered the awful heated words from that night. The ones that had excommunicated her and her mother from the lives of all but one of the Liassidis family.

'What do you want me to do?'

'I want you to go back in time and not have done it in the first place!'

'Don't be so juvenile, Leo.'

*'I want—*the board *wants—you to sell back your shares and leave Liassidis Shipping completely. And then? I want never to see you again.'*

More words and more anger had filled the room that night, all of which had been shocking to the sixteen-year-old, already grieving Helena, so much so that she rarely thought about it. Leander had been the only member of the Liassidises to keep in touch with her afterwards. Helena had sometimes wondered if it had started to spite Leo, but theirs was a true friendship, a bond that had strengthened into one of love. Just not *that* kind of love.

In her heart, she'd always believed that Leander and Kate would make the perfect couple but, despite all her best intentions to get the two together, they had only met last week when she and Kate had travelled to Greece for the wedding.

But they'd had such a great week together, Helena thought. So she couldn't understand what had caused

Leander to disappear. It hurt that he'd not been able to tell her. Leander was her friend, one she loved like a brother. Yet, instead, he'd chosen to rely on the person he hadn't spoken to for five years.

'And now we welcome Mr and Mrs Liassidis to the dance floor for their first dance as husband and wife!' exclaimed the wedding planner, pulling her awkwardly back to the present.

Leo had stood and was gesturing her towards the dance floor and suddenly she wanted to be anywhere but here. She didn't care about the money, she didn't care if she failed as the charity's CEO. She just couldn't be this close to Leonidas Liassidis, who had made it painfully clear how much he disliked even the thought of touching her.

But she didn't have a choice.

They approached the dance floor as the opening bars of *At Last* by Etta James played out across the reception hall and she determined to get through it without incident. But when she placed her hand in his and he slipped his arm around her waist, his palm splaying delicately at her back, a shiver rippled through her. He couldn't have missed it, yet his focus was firmly, almost disdainfully, on the guests.

And, just like that, she was a fifteen-year-old girl again and he was the older boy she had a crush on. The one whose girlfriend had spat venom and caused her friend to become a cold stranger. One who couldn't bear to even look at her.

'And you thought I was going to be the one having trouble keeping up this façade,' he whispered and it was all the warning she got before he pulled her against his chest, much to the tittering delight of the guests watching.

Her breasts pushed against his firm chest, the outline of his body indelibly inked on her skin, the heat of his palm on her back pressing her gently against him, keeping her there even if she could have pulled herself back.

How could her body betray her so? Her pulse leapt to his touch, arousal filling her core with an ache that was indecent. She leaned back to glare up at him but was struck by the unflinching intensity in his gaze. His eyes glowed, shards of gold pulsing deep within the rich mahogany of his gaze.

Could it be that he felt it too? The wicked energy in the air between them. The *want*.

In response to the shift in their positions, his hand curved around her ribcage, the tips of his fingers perilously close to the underside of her breast. She felt the flush of heat on her cheeks and hoped that no one could see as he bent his head to the shell of her ear.

'Just think of all the money I'm going to give you,' he whispered, returning her earlier taunt back to her. And, just like that, whatever sweet heat had built in her body flamed to ash. He had misread her body's reaction as anger? Had *she* been fool enough to misread his anger as something else entirely?

Perhaps it was better that way, because he was right. She *did* need to think of the money he was going to give her. Money that she would use to save the charity that had once saved her. She used that thought to give her strength. She needed to get access to those shares. And to do that she needed this marriage to seem real.

Leo clenched his jaw, bracing against the impact of soft, warm hands on his body. He might not remember the last time he'd held a woman like this, but he knew it hadn't felt so…incendiary.

He'd not quite been able to give his trust to another woman after the breakdown of his engagement to Mina, but that hadn't stopped him from engaging in mutually pleasurable affairs with women who valued discretion and honesty.

Helena was as far from those two things as he could imagine. But as she pressed one hand against his heart and raised the other to curl her fingers in his hair, his body didn't care that it was a calculated move for appearances' sake.

And his mind and heart wrestled between pulling her closer and pushing her away.

He risked a glance down at her, a flash of silver catching his attention. He nearly tripped when he caught sight of the silver necklace Helena wore.

'Leo…' Helena whispered, her grip tightening on his hand.

Pasting on a bright smile for the guests, he shrugged and twirled her away from him and back to buy his racing thoughts some time to calm.

'What is it?' Helena asked, settling back into the rhythm of the music, her face flushed from the dance.

'I'm surprised you're wearing that today.'

Helena's gaze snapped back to his, holding just a little

too long before she looked away, cutting him off before he could discern her thoughts.

'My necklace? Why wouldn't I? It was a gift. From Leander.'

From Leander?

And, just like that, he remembered. He remembered how his brother, at home during one of his rare visits since he'd left, had ended up claiming responsibility for the Christmas present he'd bought the fifteen-year-old Helena all those years ago.

The box, with the inscription 'From L', had contained a simple peony pendant that Leo had bought her, because they were her favourite flower. But on that last Christmas they'd all spent together—before her father had passed, before Gwen had nearly ruined their company—the argument he'd had with Mina had made it impossible for him to claim responsibility for it.

While everyone had oohed and ahhed over the pretty pendant Helena had received, Mina had already been fuming—smarting over the fact that the small blue box he'd given her contained earrings rather than the engagement ring she'd been expecting. She would have made a scene of epic proportions if she'd discovered that it was he who had bought the necklace for Helena. And in what had perhaps been their last moment of twin sense, Leander had stepped in to help him and taken credit for the present.

'It's a peony,' Helena explained, as if he didn't already know.

'Mmm,' was all Leo was capable of replying. It was something he'd completely forgotten about.

'Something old,' Helena continued. 'I guess blue is

the feeling I got when Leander didn't appear and 'new' would be you? Or would you be borrowed?' Helena said, smiling sadly.

'Borrowed would be the shares,' he snapped, feeling utterly thrown by the memories beginning to resurface.

'Of course,' Helena replied, fake smile back in place, while her eyes glowed with accusations and recriminations. 'Because you insist on conveniently forgetting that my father helped Giorgos not only found Liassidis Shipping, but also broker many of the deals that made it an international success in the first place. Your revisionist history wouldn't account for that, would it?' she demanded hotly through her teeth.

'Revisionist history?' he demanded, intensely disliking how well her verbal blow had struck.

As the song drew to an end, Helena's fingers tightened at his neck. The smile trembled for just a second before firming.

'We're done here,' Helena promised and slipped from his embrace, waving to the guests as she exited the reception through a door where Kate waited anxiously.

He was left for a moment, standing in the middle of an empty dance floor, one hundred and fifty pairs of eyes on him and none meaning a single thing to him.

'Be me.'

Leo forced a broad smile to his lips, took a comically dramatic bow and returned to the table, needing as much space from Helena as she apparently needed from him.

The whirr of the helicopter blades filled Helena's ears and she welcomed it. Welcomed the way it blocked out her chaotic thoughts and filled the silence that had descended over Leo the moment they had left the reception.

Helena had bid a tearful goodbye to Kate, unsure whether she'd get to see her best friend again before she travelled to Borneo and hating that the parting had been so focused on Leander.

God, she hoped that Kate would find him. Being around Leo was stressful enough. Every time she looked at him, all she could think of was how he was all but blackmailing her for her shares. If she hadn't been so desperate there was no way she'd have ever agreed to such a low price. Not as a grieving daughter and not as a grown businesswoman.

'We're coming in to land,' informed the pilot on the open channel in the headsets.

Helena nodded to show her understanding. She'd warned Leo already not to say anything revealing on the open channel—the pilot knew Leander well—and Leo had apparently taken that to heart by not saying a single thing. Instead, he'd spent the entire journey looking out of the window, his expression grimly guarded.

They came to land on the small helipad at the back of the beautiful Mani Peninsula villa. Their suitcases had been sent ahead earlier that morning so their belongings would be waiting for them, and all Helena could think about was getting out of her dress. It was beautiful, quite possibly the most exquisite thing she'd ever worn, but it was too much now.

The co-pilot slipped out from the front of the helicopter and slid the door open for her, holding out his hand.

Helena gratefully took it, wanting to leave Leo in the damn machine to fly off God knew—or cared—where.

Kate was gone, Leander was gone, and she was alone with the bastard who had bartered her inheritance for a pittance.

Now that the guests were far behind her, now that the stress of the day was nearly done, she could barely keep the tears back as she hurried towards the villa Leander had booked with her in mind.

'It will be our refuge for the week. Here you can finally let go and just be yourself.'

But it wasn't. It wasn't a refuge but a prison, and she couldn't let go at all—not even for one second. Because Leonidas Liassidis would be there, waiting around every corner.

'Where are you going?' Leo asked, his tone unusually blank.

She felt his gaze on her as she grabbed the bottle of champagne from where it had been placed in an ice bucket by the open front door.

'To bed. Alone. With this,' she said, holding up the green bottle, purposely keeping her back to him as the first tear rolled down her cheek.

CHAPTER FOUR

HELENA WOKE UP feeling awful. She peered at the clock on the side table next to the large bed she barely remembered collapsing into last night. She closed her eyes against the glowing display announcing that it was seven in the morning and cursed.

The last thing she remembered was promising herself that she'd just close her eyes for a short nap, but she'd slept for twelve hours. For most people that would probably be a good sign, but for Helena Hadden? Sleep was her stress response. Her body's default protection setting, a primal act of self-preservation that should have been warning enough.

She passed a hand over her face and hauled herself unsteadily to sit on the side of the bed, surprised by the cool touch of platinum from her wedding ring glancing over her skin.

Married. She was, for all intents and purposes, now married to Leander Liassidis.

Only it wasn't Leander who was here with her, but his twin brother.

Not that it mattered. Because as long as the press continued to believe that it was Leander with her, then she still had a chance to make this marriage believable. And as long as it was believable she could still save Incendia.

That thought kept her going while she showered and dressed in a long cream muslin dress, reminding herself that Leo wouldn't much care how she looked. She walked out onto the balcony of her room, the view of the Mediterranean Sea a dramatic display of sheer beauty, glittering like diamonds on silk rippled by the wind. Raising her face to the sun, she inhaled the sea salt and rosemary that always reminded her of Greece.

Her heart said *home*, but her head chided her for being fanciful.

What part did Greece play in her desire to be a successful CEO and businesswoman? To prove herself worthy of her father's name? What part did Greece play in her life when everything she knew now was in England?

But that wasn't true, was it? Not any more. Kate would soon be in Borneo, and Helena would be alone. But she told herself that it would only give her more time to focus on Incendia. On its future success *after* she had ensured they passed the financial review at the end of the year.

She sighed and prised open her eyes, the sound of something down below drawing her attention. There, powering through the gentle waters of an infinity pool that merged so well with the sea beyond she'd not even seen it, was Leo.

Dark head of hair, seal slick, and powerful muscles undulating across his back, his arms parted the water like a sea god. The glory of his easy movements, the breath he took with each alternate stroke, the backs of his thighs, the cut of his calf muscles, defined, solid, slid through the water with enough grace to barely mark the surface of the pool.

Her cheeks warming and her pulse flaring, she could no longer deny her body's response to him. It wasn't anger that made her heart pound painfully in her chest. It wasn't resentment that caused heat to burn through what little common sense she had when it came to him. The effect Leo had on her was overwhelming. The throb between her legs, the dampness even. No one had *ever* made her feel this way.

But the person she wanted to be with, to give herself to, would do more than make her body sing. They would make her feel loved, cherished, wanted because she was enough, just as she was.

And that could, she assured herself, never be the man currently in the pool below. Because the cold and aloof Leo Liassidis only wanted one thing from her: her shares. And once he got them he would leave her life, just like he had before—without a backward glance or a second thought.

Leo had devastated her teenage years and she wouldn't let that happen to her twenties. So she would stay out of his way until she couldn't avoid him any more.

Leo hauled himself from the side of the pool for the second day in a row, after eventually realising that, no matter how many times a day he swam, no matter how many laps he did, it wouldn't resolve the frustration that had plagued him for the last two days.

Helena's absence suggested that she was hiding from him. Which, if he were being honest, suited him just fine. He'd taken several meetings online both the day before and earlier that afternoon but, despite insisting that very little needed to be changed, his assistant had, for the duration of Leo's absence, taken it upon himself to 'lighten his load'.

And he didn't like it one bit. Over the years he'd developed a routine that he was happy with, that worked for both him and Liassidis Shipping. Full days and ferocious focus to the exclusion of all else was what had saved the company once, and what ensured that it was still at the top of its field today.

Leo rolled his shoulders, relishing the ache brought by his morning swim as he stood there staring out at a view that looked similar to the one from his parents' island. He hadn't been back there for quite some time now. Before, he would have blamed it on work. But was that true? Or had he just been trying to avoid his brother?

Whether it was Helena, seeing his parents at the wedding, or a strange mixture of both, his memory was tiptoeing around things he'd rather forget.

'Have you made your decision?'

'Yes, Patéra. I'm going to work at Liassidis Shipping.'

At eighteen, he'd been so excited to accept the mantle his father was willing to pass on. Wanting to make him proud. Wanting to work with his brother, to stand by his side as they became men.

'And you, Leander?'

'I...' He'd not even been able to look Leo in the eye. *'I want to take the money.'*

Leo clenched his jaw, braced against the memory of that day. But, in truth, it wasn't that moment that had been the fatal blow to his relationship with Leander. It had been the days, weeks, months of daydreams leading up to it. Of his brother pretending to support his plans for their future. The *years* of believing that he and his brother shared one thought, one desire, one goal.

And none of it had been real.

It had been him alone in that daydream. And him alone to bear the weight of the damage caused by Gwen three years later. By that point, he hadn't even expected or wanted Leander to come home to help. But it had also been him alone to pull Liassidis Shipping back from the brink of absolute disaster.

And it had taught him an invaluable lesson. If he couldn't rely on his twin, he couldn't rely on anyone. And he'd honed that independence into a skill. That way, he didn't have distractions, he didn't leave himself or his company open to other people's incompetence or betrayal. No. It was far better for him to go it alone.

Leo shook off the water from his hair and dried himself with a towel when his mobile beeped. He stopped to check the message.

We have the gallery event.

Frowning at the message from Helena that could just have easily been said in person, he typed back irritably.

Yes?

The car is coming in thirty minutes.

His hackles rippled at her clipped tone, but he restrained the urge to snipe back. Yes, Helena needed him. But he also needed her. If he alienated her, he might never get hold of those shares, and he'd never have what he'd always wanted: complete control of Liassidis Shipping.

He reached his room and peered at the wardrobe, filled with clothes that belonged to his brother. Clearly, when Leander had left, it had been with nothing but his phone and presumably a passport.

But the moment Leo caught himself wondering what had possibly made his brother do such a thing, he stopped himself. It made no difference to him. He no longer allowed himself to be tormented by the whys of his brother's behaviour.

He showered quickly, dressed and was buttoning up the crisp white shirt when he realised he was standing in the one place in his room where he could see through his own door, down the hallway and into Helena's room.

From this exact point, he could see the corner of her bed, and Helena looking at her reflection in a floor-length mirror.

Leo turned his attention to the cuffs of his sleeves. At home, Leo had rows and rows of cufflinks on display. They were the final touch on an appearance that mattered to him as the face of Liassidis Shipping. And while Leo knew Leander wouldn't wear them, he purposefully retrieved the pair he'd worn the day he'd arrived at the wedding and fastened them in place.

He glanced back up to catch Helena putting in an earring. Her head was tilted to one side, her hair styled in a pretty, messy knot high on her head, showing off the slender arch of her neck. It was such a simple moment, but one that felt oddly private, as if it were something he shouldn't be witnessing.

But his gaze still consumed the sight of her, dressed in the floor-length, high-necked green velvet dress, as if she were a feast. His hungry imagination, delighting in this moment of voyeurism, offered up suggestions for what his eyes couldn't see and what his subconscious desperately wanted.

Inches of pale skin glowing beneath jade-coloured lingerie filled his mind. He saw his hand slide across that skin, felt it shiver beneath his touch, tasted the heady scent of her as he pressed open-mouthed kisses to her breasts, relished the damp, wet heat of her as he delved between her legs.

His pulse tripped and sweat broke out across his neck. Locked in that moment of erotic images, his famously quick brain made a million and one connections, all hurtling towards fierce arousal as if it were a race.

So attuned to her body, he felt the moment she realised that he was watching her, the way that tension pulled like a thread across her shoulders. He forced his gaze away and stepped from view, taking ruthless control over his wayward body.

Helena was a means to an end. Nothing more. She could never be anything more. And he didn't *want* anything more, he told himself. This was nothing but an aberrant response to the female form. And it wouldn't happen again, he warned himself.

By the time he'd regained his composure, Helena had retrieved her clutch and was making her way towards him down the corridor.

'You shouldn't be wearing cufflinks.'

Biting back a response, because right now anything that came out of his mouth would either sound petulant or lecherous, he simply stated, 'We'll be late.'

'Leander is always late,' she dismissed easily. 'You shouldn't be wearing cufflinks.'

'I should be about two hundred and eighty kilometres away and not here, involved in this farce, but...' And he shrugged as if to say, *here we are.*

Helena glared at him. 'Fine. But please remember. If people don't believe that you are Leander and that we are happily married, you can kiss your shares goodbye.'

The car pulled up at the red-carpeted entrance to the gallery in Kalamata for the opening night of an exhibition by an up-and-coming artist garnering deserved amounts of attention for her unique subversion of the male gaze. Helena had been more than happy to support the event when Leander had chosen it, but with Leo beside her she wanted to be anywhere else but here.

She just couldn't imagine how he would respond to the detailed and graphic images that had prompted extreme responses in both the media and the public. But, Helena supposed, she would soon find out.

Leo slipped wordlessly from the car and came round to her door, holding it open and offering his hand. The smile on his face shocked her for a moment after the cold silence between them since leaving the villa, but then the first of many flashbulbs erupted and she remembered that he was supposed to be Leander.

She stood and he placed her hand in the crook of his arm and gestured towards the length of red carpet, where the three-deep crowd of paparazzi waited impatiently. As always, she felt assaulted by the bright flashes of light directed their way. In England, her family wealth and name had always drawn attention, but her marriage to a Liassidis had launched the attention into a whole new stratosphere.

'Leander, over here!'

'Helena, Helena!' another called.

From somewhere in the mass of dark shapes looming behind the bright flashes, questions were hurled their way.

'How's the honeymoon going, Helena?' one voice jeered, but she kept her smile.

'Is it true what they say about him, Helena?'

She swallowed at the crass comments, distaste and disgust crawling over her skin. She felt the flex of Leo's forearm beneath her palm. Unlike his brother, Leo had never courted the press. Especially not after the months and months of speculation and derision at his leadership fail in the early stages of taking over Liassidis Shipping. A hounding scrutiny that he had protected her mother from, even as he'd engineered her removal from the company.

'Helena, are you here for pleasure, or are you hoping to gain a brand ambassador for Incendia, perhaps?'

Seizing on the sanest question of the evening, and the opportunity to increase awareness for her charity, she paused and found the reporter amongst the masses, allowing a genuine smile to spread across her features.

'I would be incredibly lucky to do so, but for tonight we're just here to enjoy the exhibition. Efi Balaskou is a fascinating artist and I can't wait to see her exhibition.'

'*Efcharistó*, Helena. Leander? If you have a moment?'

Leo's focus had been on the crowd until the mention of Incendia. She couldn't have explained why, but she felt it. His attention had zeroed in on it, as if it were a vulnerability he could take advantage of.

And the horrible truth was that it was.

'Congratulations on your wedding. It was a beautiful event.'

Leo smiled broadly, setting off another round of flashes from photographers who knew bankable good looks when they saw them.

'Oh, that little thing?' he said, full of tease that felt just wrong coming from Leo's lips. 'It was perfect, wasn't it, *agápi mou*?' he went on, turning to Helena.

She smiled, despite a strong suspicion that he'd used that term precisely because she'd told him not to.

'But your brother wasn't there. We've all heard the rumours of the rift between you, but how did it feel for him to have missed your wedding day?'

Helena's mind went blank. She just hadn't expected the question. This time, the pause, though infinitesimal, seemed to stretch out before them like eternity.

Leo narrowed his gaze at the reporter and, in a panic, Helena tightened her grip on his arm.

'You know what Leo Liassidis is like,' Leo dismissed, after an eternal moment of near deafening silence.

The reporter laughed, clearly thinking he was in on an inside joke of some sort.

'*Naí*. The words *stick up* and *backside* come to mind,' the reporter said in Greek.

Helena flushed. It was one thing to think it, but another entirely to say it. And accidentally to the man's face? Breath rippled in her chest, making her light-headed enough to want to come to Leo's defence.

'I—'

'It would take an act of God to remove that stick,' Leo interrupted, leaning towards the reporter conspiratorially. 'He had *very important business*,' Leo mimicked and for a moment Helena was so lost in Leo being Leander, being Leo, that she simply stared at him. 'I hear that he's so wedded to his office chair, he takes it home with him.'

The reporter laughed again as she forced an awkward smile to her lips.

'Helena, were you offended by your brother-in-law's absence?'

Leo looked at her, the challenge in his eyes wicked. As if he were saying, *Now's your chance.* A wickedness that cut through the years, the bitter recriminations between them, to before her mother's mistake, before the loss of her father, before that horrible Christmas, to when she'd felt safe in their relationship, when she'd felt she'd known him. And that he'd known her.

'I'm usually more offended by his presence, so for

me his absence made a pleasant change,' she announced loftily, holding Leo's gaze.

Leo threw his head back and laughed. A genuine, full-throated laugh that caught almost everyone's attention.

She couldn't help but let a smile curve her lips. It wasn't every day she managed to score a point against Leo Liassidis, but to make him laugh like that? Like he used to? A round of flashes went off and it was as if the stars had fallen from the sky to land at their feet. Leo recovered himself and gestured for her to continue down the carpet and she followed, dazzled not by the lights but by *him*.

Leo hadn't expected to laugh. He'd expected to be angry. He'd expected to use her as a foil to vent his frustrations. But she'd surprised him. And he hadn't been surprised for a very long time. He strangely welcomed the moment to move beyond all the anger from the past, even if just for a while.

They navigated the small bottleneck blocking the entrance to the gallery and each accepted a glass of champagne from the wait staff. Making sure that there were no reporters hidden behind corners waiting to catch him out, he finally took a sip of his drink as he turned back to the larger-than-life photograph they stood before and promptly choked.

Bubbles ran simultaneously down his throat and up his nose, blocking off his airways.

There was a distinctly unsympathetic smirk across Helena's features as, without taking her eyes from the gallery piece, she passed him a napkin. Leo's eyes watered as he vainly tried to contain all the liquid trying to leave his body at the same time, while he avoided the image that had caused this disastrous incident in the first place.

'Helena, what the hell have you brought me to?' he whispered the moment he regained the ability to speak.

'It is called art, Lee—Leander,' she managed, spinning his name into his brother's in case anyone was listening.

'That,' he spat, 'is pornography.' It didn't seem to matter that he'd glanced at the photograph for less than a second—the image was indelibly inked on his brain. But, what was worse, it was now irrevocably linked to Helena.

Gamóto.

The last thing he wanted, or needed, was to be thinking of Helena in any correlation to the image of a pair of lips utterly encasing a rather turgid part of the male anatomy, in such close proximity that the photographer made the viewer feel less observer and more participant.

One quick glance around the other images adorning clean white gallery walls confirmed his fears. They were everywhere. Every possible sexual act imaginable seemed to be blown up in extreme detail and pasted all over every wall. He could turn a corner and fall headfirst into a *ménage à trois* if he wasn't careful.

'I didn't take you for such a prude.'

'I'm not,' he assured her. 'In the privacy of my own bedroom.'

And suddenly the air thickened between them, heavy

with the implication of what *did* happen in his bedroom. Helena's teasing lips wobbled a little. Lips that he had swiped with the pad of his thumb. Lips that he now associated with the large photograph directly behind her. And it was as if that thought lit the touchpaper that had been the last barrier of his restraint.

Helena broke the connection between them, taking slow steps from one large canvas to another. Amongst the black and white images on display and the monochromatic style of the other guests, she stood out like a shard of jade. He followed behind her, stalking her, past pictures of increasingly detailed sexual acts that merged with his earlier fantasies about the woman mere inches away from him. It was a very fine line and he was hovering dangerously close.

'You look like you're angry with me,' she said, her gaze in a reflection of glass covering a sculpture of twisting limbs in marble.

'How do you want me to look at you?' he asked before he could stop himself, the question unspooling a dangerous arousal between them.

She stilled, the pulse flickering at her throat daring him to push further, the tremble of her fingers on the stem of the champagne flute urging him beyond his usual self-control.

'Like I'm your newly married husband?' he pressed, leaning over her shoulder to whisper into the shell of her ear, unable to help himself. 'Like I want to do these things to you?'

The sharp inhalation of her shock was both a warning and a temptation, but when she stepped away from the heat of his body he let her go. He took a mouthful of the champagne but it did nothing to cool the ardent heat coursing across his skin.

What was wrong with him?

There was too much at stake to play silly games like that. He blamed it on his body's primal reaction to her as a woman, the shocking difference between the girl he'd once known and the incredibly beautiful adult before him. He then spent the next twenty minutes wandering the gallery as far from her as possible while he struggled for the control that he was so famous for.

By the time he'd reined himself in he found Helena standing by the window that looked over a stunning Greek nightscape.

'When can we leave?' he asked, clearing his throat.

'Soon,' she said without looking at him. And he was thankful that at least one of them had sense enough to maintain the barriers between them.

He took another careful sip of his champagne, searching for something safe for them to discuss, rather than the dangerously sensual play they should most definitely not be engaging in.

'What is Incendia?' he asked, expecting her to respond with some bland explanation of her day job.

He knew Helena well enough that the evasive shoulder shrug and moue she made with her lips was as red a flag as any.

He nodded to himself and pulled out his phone.

'What are you doing?' she asked, turning her attention finally away from the view from the gallery window.

'Looking up Incendia.'

She pushed down his phone with a sharp slap of her hand, catching him completely by surprise, red slashes on her cheekbones, and not through pleasure but anger.

'What do you want to know?' she demanded in a low voice.

'What you're trying to hide,' he returned, just as low, sliding his phone back into his suit pocket.

Helena had never been one for deceit and, on reflection, even the idea that she would actually marry Leander to access money was so uncharacteristic he couldn't believe he hadn't seen it before.

'I'm not trying to hide anything,' she said with a shrug. 'I'm CEO of Incendia, a—'

'Oh, Christ, Helena, don't tell me you're trying to prop it up with your own money,' he interrupted, his hand bracketing his temples.

The shock in her gaze, the fear as she looked around to make sure that no one had heard him, made him even more furious.

She grabbed him by the arm and pulled him into a corridor away from the main exhibition.

Anger crawled up and bit into whatever peace had been found between them as he yanked his arm back. What she was doing was immature and reckless. Dangerous even, and not just for her company but for herself.

'Didn't you learn anything from your mother?' he demanded.

'My mother made a mistake,' Helena hissed. 'She thought she had learned enough about business from listening to my father for years. And you punished her terribly for it.'

The accusation was both unjust and true at the same time, but Leo couldn't leave it at that.

'She didn't just make a mistake, Helena. She expressly went against the wishes of not just me but the entire board of Liassidis Shipping. She engaged one client—a fierce competitor of an existing one—to make herself feel like a businesswoman, and nearly bankrupted us in the process.'

Helena's defiance faltered. It was just a second, but it was enough.

'You didn't know that?' he asked, before he could take it back.

'I knew enough!' Helena cried. 'I was there when you yelled at her and called her stupid, and foolish, and a liability. She was a grieving woman, Leo,' she accused, 'and you cut her off from everything and everyone she knew.'

'And you're still making excuses for her,' he hit back, wondering if she would ever stop searching for something that Gwen would never give her.

'She's my mother,' Helena replied, unable to stop herself from feeling all the hurt, anger and confusion from that time building up all over again. When everything she had known had been slipping through her fingers—she'd lost her father, her mother had made a terrible mistake and then Leo was pushing them out of his and his family's lives as if they were nothing more than an inconvenience.

'Then how could you possibly even contemplate making the same mistake again? If the company is failing, it's failing,' he announced with a fatal finality.

'It's not failing,' she slammed back. 'It's employee theft. All we need to do is survive the financial review at the end of the year,' she insisted.

Leo shook his head, that same look of disappointment in his eyes now that she remembered from when her mother had messed up.

'You cannot put your own money at risk like this,' he warned.

'Why not? *You* did,' she accused.

'Because it was *my* company, Helena. This? It's just a job. A CEO's position.'

'Even if it *was* just that, why is it okay for you to do it but not okay for me?'

And that was when she saw it. The answer that she feared the most.

'Because you think I'll fail,' she correctly interpreted. A sob rose in her chest. To see him staring back at her, disappointed and disapproving, it was her worst imaginings come to life. 'Thank you for your vote of confidence, Leo.'

She pushed past him and out of the gallery, the cool of the night biting into her heated emotions. As she messaged the car service, she told herself that Leo was wrong. She wouldn't mess this up. She would save Incendia and prove him wrong. She knew what she was doing. All she had to do was stick to the plan and it would work. She knew it would.

Her phone buzzed in her clutch and she read the message from Kate with a strange mix of relief and resentment. And felt immediately bad. Her best friend had travelled halfway round the world to help her. Leander had to be in some sort of trouble to have done what he'd done. And all she could think of was that it wasn't enough.

Oh, why was this such a mess?

Leo came to stand beside her just as the car pulled up.

'Kate's found Leander.'

'Hopefully, she can bring him back before it's too late,' Leo said.

But Helena feared it already was.

CHAPTER FIVE

WHO OPENED A club on a Wednesday night? Leo wondered as he looked at the wardrobe with neatly pinned paper cards informing the wearer of the date and the event. Leander's assistant needed a pay rise. Leo would never have asked his to do such a thing.

He doesn't have to, because you never go out, a distinctly Helena-sounding voice said in his head.

Leo rubbed a hand over the closely cut beard on his jaw. It had been two days since the gallery opening. Two days before that had been the wedding. If it followed this pattern, he could avoid Helena for another two days, starting tomorrow.

Because you'll say some other appalling thing to her and cause her more upset.

That voice sounded like his brother.

The fact that Leo had been right about everything he'd said that night at the gallery hadn't quietened his conscience. If anything, it had only got louder and louder as time wore on. He'd catch glimpses of Helena around the villa, the trail of a scarf, or a pair of sunglasses lying around. A book she'd left on a lounger that he'd been curious about and looked up. Little pieces of a girl he'd once known.

At least their argument had drawn a line under whatever had invaded his senses that day. Not that he'd forgotten the words he'd whispered to her, how close he'd come to crossing the invisible line between them. He assured himself that he was cured of that momentary madness as he considered the deep ochre-coloured T-shirt and dark maroon linen suit Leander's assistant had chosen for tonight. A pair of sunglasses were tucked by an arm into the breast pocket and a leather belt hung over the suit shoulder. He frowned at the casual attire.

'Be me.'

Kill me, thought Leo as he reached for the clothes that would turn him into Leander.

As he buttoned his shirt and tucked it into the waistband of his trousers, he racked his brain for why he had suddenly become so responsive to Helena. Yes, it had been a while since he'd last spent time with someone.

But after Mina he'd had absolutely no intention of making himself that vulnerable again. Since then, women had been an *as and when* for him and certainly no more permanent than a night or two of mutual pleasure. Despite his reaction to the pictures in the gallery, he wasn't a prude. Far from it. He enjoyed pleasure, his partner's and his own, greatly. He just didn't have to splash it all over the papers like his brother.

With one last look in the mirror, he went to the living room, to find Helena looking at her watch.

'So "Leander the Lothario" wanted to take you to a club opening on your honeymoon,' he stated, trying to warm the chill in the air between them and ease his conscience at the same time.

'Travi, the owner of the club, is a business associate,' she informed him in a clipped tone that he should be thankful for.

'Of yours?' Leo asked, confused.

'Of *Leander's*,' Helena replied disdainfully, as if she were reproving him for how little he knew about his brother's life.

As if it were *he* that had caused the separation between them.

'I thought Leander is into web-based app development.'

'He is. Travi is an investor.'

As they left the villa and made their way to the helipad where the helicopter would fly them back to Athens for the evening, the blush-pink sparkles covering Helena's dress glistened in the setting sun. Before him was a kaleidoscope of golds, yellows and pinks that struck him in full Technicolor. Where the dress from the previous event had been long, this one stopped barely at where her fingers reached her toned thighs.

He clenched his jaw and slipped the sunglasses over his eyes.

'So, you know Travi well?' he asked as he followed, trying to watch where he was going and not the backs of Helena's well-defined thighs.

'Reasonably. But not as much as Leander. You're going to have to concentrate this time.'

He nodded, though he already knew that hemline was going to be a major problem.

'I'm surprised you know so much about my brother,' he observed out loud.

'I'm surprised you know so little,' she snapped back in a rebuke he felt to his core.

The helicopter was waiting for them, the door slid back and the blades at a standstill for the moment. He waited while they took their seats and the headsets were in place. The co-pilot talked them through what channels to use and what to do in an emergency and Leo only heard every other word over the pounding in his head as the vee of Helena's dress gaped just enough to reveal the gentle slope of her breast.

Skatá, he was turning into a pervert.

'We kept in touch.' Helena's words came through the headset, bringing him back to their conversation.

He didn't miss the unspoken accusation that *he* hadn't bothered to keep in touch with her.

You cut her off from everything and everyone she knew.

Had Helena just been talking about her mother? Or had she also been talking about herself?

'Do you see him regularly?' Leo asked, choosing his words carefully, wondering how much of an answer he really wanted.

Helena smiled and her face lit up. 'We find time to celebrate the milestones. I don't get to come to Greece that often any more, so he'll usually fly to London. He was...' she looked up at him and then away '...there when I needed him.'

The sting of jealousy surprised Leo and it covered everything. Not just the fact that Leander was there for Helena in a way that Leander had never been there for him. But because there had once been a time when Helena had come to *him* and not Leander. And the way she talked about what they had made him curious about the man he'd cut from his life.

'Is he happy?' Leo asked, unsure of the answer he wanted to hear.

Helena looked at him from across the helicopter. 'Yes,' she said with a small smile. 'But sometimes I get a sense that there's something missing from his life.'

'What?' Leo couldn't help but ask.

'You.'

He couldn't say anything to that.

Helena felt unusually self-conscious entering the trendy nightclub owned by Travi Samaras. People turned to stare, but she was under no illusion as to who it was that drew their attention. She was standing next to a man who looked like a Greek god worshipped by mortals, rather than one himself.

She would have laughed had she been with Leander, but standing beside Leo, seeing the impact he had on other women, feeling the impact he had on her *without even trying*, was making her feel distinctly on edge.

'What's wrong? Are you nervous?' he asked, dipping his head to her ear, once again playing the doting new husband.

'No. Just curious as to how on earth you're going to succeed in pretending to be your party animal brother,' she replied, wondering how he'd noticed her discomfort.

'You don't think I know how to party?' came the amusingly indignant reply.

'I don't think you'd know a good time if it came up and slapped you across the face,' she said as she stalked towards the bar. He kept pace with her as she made her way through a sea of people that parted for Leo as if he were Moses.

'I do,' he insisted as he reached her side at the bar.

'You *did*,' she countered, his persistence softening some of her defiance.

'What's that supposed to mean?'

She deliberately caught the eye of the barman rather than look up at Leo, whose famous focus was now intently on her.

She shrugged. 'Once upon a time you knew how to have fun. Now? Not so much.' Turning a smile on the barman, she ordered a bottle of champagne.

'You can put it on Leander Liassidis' tab,' she told the barman sweetly.

Leo's eyes widened in realisation, his lips curving into a wicked smile just before asking the barman to make it two bottles.

'Just the two?' Helena asked as she found a standing table at the edge of a dance floor while the bar staff set up tall buckets with ice and two glasses.

'I'm ordering a bottle of vodka next,' he growled.

Helena found herself smiling despite herself. The merest hint of the boy she remembered from her childhood was enough to warm her. Back then, he'd been funny, irreverent. More grounded than Leander, yes, but so much less serious and sombre than the adult Leo.

She was about to reply when she saw Travi making his way towards them.

'The man in the white suit and dark shirt? That's Travi. You've known him for three years, ever since he approached you looking for an investor,' she whispered hurriedly. 'You decided against the first project, but liked an app designed by one of his young techs and invested in that instead. You tried to pinch the tech, but Travi made him an offer he couldn't refuse to stay. You said at the end, *At least the kid is finally being paid his worth.* You joke about it regularly.'

Leo stared at her, his gaze halfway between surprised and impressed.

'What?' she asked, wondering what she'd done, but before she could ask, Travi had arrived at their table.

'So, you incorrigible flirt, you finally bit the bullet and settled down with this unimpeachable goddess who is worth ten of your weight in gold,' Travi announced, grabbing Leo by the shoulders and nearly wrestling him into a headlock.

Helena pressed a hand against her mouth to try to stop her laugh escaping from the shock on Leo's face, until he managed to regain his composure, or at least recall that he was supposed to be Leander.

'Hey, *maláka*, I know exactly how much she's worth,' he said, turning in the man's hold to accept the hug in a way that seemed utterly alien to Leo, but absolutely one hundred percent Leander. '*Everything.* She's worth everything.'

Although Leo was looking at Travi, the words struck Helena hard, catching her breath in her chest. Because wasn't that what she'd always wanted? To be someone's everything.

'But if you call her goddess again, we're going to have words,' Leo added with a warning bite that sounded foreign to her ears as she hastily pushed down the sudden bloom in her heart.

'Helena, *angeli mou*, light of my life, why did you pick him? You know I would have married you in a heartbeat,' the other Greek male complained.

'Travi,' she said, taking his face in her hands, the smile on her face only a little forced. 'You know how much I love you, but he has a bigger bank account,' she teased.

'How very dare you?' Travi cried in a high falsetto and a cut glass English accent. 'I expect you both to be the last couple standing,' he commanded with a finger pointed right at them, before he left to meet and greet his other guests.

One after the other, many familiar faces from amongst Leander's crowd came and went, Leo seemingly relaxed and easy, mimicking his brother so well that even Helena nearly forgot. But it wasn't just the smiles and jokes. Talk quite often turned to business—and she suddenly realised how many of Leander's acquaintances he'd actually met through business. Someone needing investment advice, or wanting the 'in' on his latest app development.

Leo handled each and every one with an ease and confidence that surprised her, the marked difference from the man who could barely bring himself to touch her at the wedding, who was more relaxed and freer somehow.

When someone tapped her on the shoulder she turned and found herself immediately wrapped in the warm embrace of Serene, a friend of Leander and Travi that she'd spent some time with in London when she'd visited for work.

'Man, you tamed the devil,' Serene teased in English, nodding to Leo and mistaking him, just like everyone else, for Leander. 'I didn't think anything would make him settle down.'

'Neither did I,' Helena replied, feeling a little guilty for the deception now that she was with friends.

'So, what is it like?' Serene demanded as Helena passed her a champagne flute. 'Married life! Gah, I can't think of anything worse.'

Others around the table joined in the conversation, affectionately shouting her down, but Serene remained beautifully and happily adamant.

'Go on,' she taunted Helena. 'Hit me with it. What's the best thing about being newlyweds?'

'Oh, I don't know...' Helena hedged. 'Morning breath?' she offered, determined to hold onto the humour in the conversation.

'Picking up someone else's dirty laundry,' another of Leander's friends contributed.

'Argh.' Serene grimaced, the look of horror on her face comical.

'Having to put the toilet seat back down,' another woman added.

'Okay, no. If you're not going to be serious about this,

then I'll ask him. Hey!' she shouted, pulling at Leo's arm. 'What's so great about being married, Leander?'

Leo looked at the expectant faces around the table. He knew they'd all been laughing about it, but as he looked at Helena he didn't want to laugh it off. He had once believed in the sanctity of marriage. He'd wanted it, hoped for it. Thought he'd nearly had it. Helena's smile faltered just a little and he forced a smile to his lips.

'The best part about being newly married is that I get to dance with my wife whenever I want!' he said, reaching for her and pulling her away from the crowd to the celebratory yells and encouragement of Leander's friends.

As he led her to the dance floor Leo felt drained from having to pretend to be his brother for the last two hours. He hadn't realised how at the wedding no one had actually said anything more than congratulations. And at the gallery they hadn't spoken to anyone after the red carpet.

But this had been different. These were Leander's friends. And Leo liked them. He could see how easy they were around each other, how supportive, how interconnected. Business was business all over the globe, so he could field any specific work-related questions with ease. The loyalty these people had to Leander—who, in Leo's considered opinion, had the staying power of cheap Sellotape—surprised him. He was struck, seeing his brother through other people's eyes. But he was also struck by how *he* was seen.

As a man who didn't show up to his brother's wedding.

A man with a stick up his backside.

A man who couldn't relax.

In truth, he was a man who couldn't remember the last time he'd come to a club or been out with his own friends, and it was that realisation that had made him want a moment away from Leander's friends, so he'd clutched at the opportunity to draw Helena on to the dance floor.

But then the music that had been full of wild beats and chaotic chords had changed and morphed into something deeper, with a bass line that rolled over the skin and senses like a promise. The track poured sibilance into the air like a thousand whispers and the hyper-awareness of earlier became almost painful.

Helena looked up at him uncertainly. She looked at him like he was Leo Liassidis, not his brother. And it was a smile he didn't want anyone else to see. He led her deeper into the dance floor to find just a little anonymity, a little breathing space, he told himself. He wanted to explain himself to Helena, why he'd brought them to the dance floor, but when he turned he realised his mistake.

Swaying to the beat of the music, she unfurled beneath the dim blue lights throbbing from above. She reached up to sweep her hair from her neck, eyes closed, her rapture was all her own and it was the most erotic thing he'd seen. Even after the gallery exhibition.

As she shifted from foot to foot, the hemline of her dress, that had been barely decent before, became nothing but temptation, sliding across thighs that he wanted to grip and pull against him. Hot pinpricks of desire broke out across his shoulders and the base of his spine. His breath was staccato in his chest.

This wasn't some artful moment of manipulation. There was no intent or thought for anyone else, he could tell. Not because she just wasn't that type of person but because her focus, one he could feel almost instinctively, was on herself. Her pure enjoyment of the moment.

Just at that moment she opened her eyes, unerringly finding him without having to search, and all the blood rushed from his head. The crowd on the dance floor grew bigger and someone jostled him, but he still couldn't look away. Just as the music built to a crescendo, the girl behind Helena careened into her from behind and Helena was thrust forward, Leo only having enough time to reach for her as she crashed against him.

Suddenly, his hands were full of soft, hot skin and sequins. Her breasts pressed against his chest, her hands, one palm to his heart, the other clinging to the lapel of his linen jacket. His breath left his lungs, and instinct took over. He pulled her more firmly against him, his fingers flexing against her body. Neither of them moved, a breath held, shared between them. Helena leaned back and this time when she looked at him there was something beneath the trepidation: *want*.

He was jostled again and the moment was cut short when she pulled out of his arms and laughed a little, perhaps at herself, perhaps at him. But whatever it was that had passed between them was over. And he couldn't work out whether that was a good thing or a bad thing.

Helena left the dance floor without looking to see if Leo was following her. She needed some time and space to sort through what had just happened. Or at least what she had just wanted to happen. She pressed the back of her hand against her flushed cheek and turned towards the table when a hand caught her wrist.

Leo looked at her with no trace of a reaction to what had just taken place on the dance floor.

'Travi wanted us in the VIP section?'

She nodded reluctantly. She wanted to go home. Not just to the villa, but *home* home. To England. But even that was no longer the refuge it had once been, everything tainted by Gregory's theft and Kate's soon-to-be absence.

She wanted to hide from everything that she was feeling, but instead she followed Leo past the suited bouncer who unhooked a red velvet twisted rope, up the stairs and over towards a red velvet sofa.

They had barely sat down when a waiter appeared with a silver bucket, a bottle of champagne and two flutes.

'With the host's congratulations on your recent nuptials.'

The flourish was so extravagant she bit back a laugh and allowed the distraction to smooth over the tension from the dance floor. Leo graciously accepted as Leander and the waiter disappeared, but he looked strangely disappointed.

'What's wrong?' she asked.

He scratched his chin and winced. 'I was hoping to buy the entire club a round of drinks. On Leander's tab, of course.'

Helena smiled. 'It would be the least he deserves. I mean the least *you* could do,' she hastily corrected.

Leo poured them each a glass and offered her one.

'A toast.'

'To?' she enquired.

He paused, looking at her a little too intently. 'To new beginnings.'

She grasped it like a lifeline but, clinking her glass to his, she couldn't hold his gaze for long. She looked down over the crowded club and wondered what that might look like.

New beginnings.

Unable to stifle her curiosity, she turned back to him, the question in her eyes finding its way to her mouth.

'What would that look like? To you?'

The hand holding his glass paused halfway to his lips, his gaze locked on hers, until it refocused on something—someone—over her shoulder.

Leo cursed.

'So, "Leander the Lothario" finally settles down?' the woman said when she arrived at their table.

Helena swallowed, genuinely incapable of speech in that moment. Panic swelled and her heartbeat thundered in her ears. She couldn't believe what she was seeing. Of all the people they could have run into.

'Mina,' Leo greeted through clenched teeth. 'What are you doing here?'

They were going to be found out. There was no way that Mina would let them leave without creating the biggest scene she possibly could.

'Don't be silly, Leander, you're not the only one who moves in these circles.'

It took a moment for Helena's brain to catch up because she genuinely couldn't believe the woman that Leo had been engaged to couldn't tell the difference between him and Leander.

'Just because your brother doesn't deign to come down off his lofty mountain to have some fun, doesn't mean that I don't. But Helena?' she said, still directing her conversation to Leo, as if even now she was beneath Mina's consideration. 'Of all people, you chose to marry *her*?'

'I'm sitting right here, Mina,' she said as calmly as she could, but her pulse was wildly erratic and her hands fisted.

'Yes, you are. But I don't understand why,' she dismissed with a shrug. 'Everyone knew you had a silly schoolgirl crush on Leo.'

Humiliation crawled up Helena's skin in angry inches, hating that Leo was sitting right there hearing everything she said. 'That was a long time ago. Things change.'

Leo cursed. There had been a time when Mina was the woman he'd wanted to spend his life with, to have a family with. Back then, he'd found her avarice amusing; it had been tempered by youth and her insecurity was much better hidden. But age had only made her worse. And that she couldn't even tell that it was him was shocking.

Mina's jealousy of Helena was as blatant as it was unpleasant. Looking back, he remembered the shame and embarrassment he'd felt at the conversation they'd had that last Christmas the two families had spent together before Helena's father had died. At the time he'd thought the feeling was because of his awareness of Helena's feelings for him. He now realised in a shocking moment of self-revelation that he'd been embarrassed by Mina. And himself, for letting her say the things that she'd said. His stomach turned and he looked at Mina, truly looked at her, trying to find some semblance of the young woman he'd spent nearly three years of his life with, but he found that there was nothing of her left.

'Things don't change that much, Lena,' Mina spat.

'Don't call her that.' His tone was as definitive and unquestionable as his swift and sudden dislike of her use of the nickname for Helena that only he had ever used. And from the look on Mina's face, she didn't like it one bit. He should have known that she'd turn on Helena in response.

'So, when you couldn't get your hands on Leo you settled for the "other" Liassidis instead?' she threw at Helena.

Leo barked a laugh and leaned back into the sofa. '*Other?* There's nothing *other* about me, darling,' he said, perfectly impersonating his brother.

'I. Don't. Believe. It,' Mina said, leaning forward, wafting alcohol over them with every word. She was drunk, Leo realised. Very drunk. 'Whatever this is,' she slurred, 'I hope you get found out.'

Warning her to keep her voice down wouldn't work in the slightest. But he couldn't let her run around thinking or, worse, saying this to others. He just had to make her believe it.

'There's nothing to find out, Mina. This is the woman

I have pledged to love for the rest of my life. And I intend to do just that,' he said, reaching for Helena and hauling her into his lap, facing him.

The look of surprise on Helena's face lasted a breath's length before understanding dawned in her gaze. He raised an eyebrow in query. If she wasn't with him in this, he'd leave her alone, he'd stop the charade and leave the club that very moment.

Subtly, Helena nodded and with his eyes on Mina's over Helena's shoulder, he brought her closer and deeper into his lap with his hands on her backside.

Helena pressed her lips together as if trying to control her response to him, but there was no controlling his response to her.

Slowly, so very slowly, he leaned towards her, wanting to give Helena time to stop him if she needed to. But she didn't. He became aware of the scent of her perfume, something heady and full of citrus, teasing his senses just as much as the heat of her body against his.

His lips were mere inches from hers and Mina no longer existed. The busy, crowded bar receded, the blood rushed in his ears and his heart pounded in his chest so violently he feared the world would hear it.

Want.

He could lie to himself, justify a kiss with the need to keep up the pretence, but he wanted this. He wanted *her*.

His lips met Helena's in what was supposed to be just a kiss. But there was nothing 'just' about it. It exploded through his body, his lips not content with a simple press, as he gently teased and prised her mouth open to

his. Her gasp—surprise or pleasure, he wasn't sure—
poured into his mouth and he was done.

He pulled back, shocked, trying to understand what
was happening, but the sight of Helena staring up at him,
wide-eyed, flushed and kiss drunk, meant he couldn't
have held back for the world. He claimed her mouth
again just as Helena's hands came to his jacket, clinging to the lapels as if needing an anchor.

Bringing his hand to cup her jaw, he angled her to him
and took full advantage of the position. Open-mouthed,
his tongue claimed her, thrusting deep into a soft, wet
heat that was instantly addictive. He plundered like a
Neanderthal, while holding himself back with a ruth-
lessness that bordered on masochism. She became fire
in his arms. Heat and passion rippled between them like
a wildfire and it was only the desire to do so much more
that brought him to his senses.

CHAPTER SIX

HELENA'S HEART POUNDED as if she'd run a marathon. Breath heaved in and out of her chest. Every part of her was vibrating at an almost invisible level, but altogether it made her whole being hum at a frequency that only Leo could ignite.

The first kiss had been a shock—an assault to her senses. She had fantasised so much and for so long that she couldn't believe it was happening.

But it was the second kiss—the one that hadn't been Leander kissing his wife, but Leo kissing her—that shifted the sands beneath her feet. It was a drugging kiss, lowering her defences and igniting her desires. His tongue stroked her into submission, filling her in a way that only partially satiated her desires, whilst igniting more. She *felt* how much he wanted her. Straddling his thighs, the hard ridge of his arousal pressed heavy and hot against her core and it wasn't nearly enough. From this position she was above him, Leo reaching for her, pulling her down onto him, and it made her feel invincible—wanted and needed in a way she'd never experienced before.

When he finally pulled back, desire blazing in his

eyes like a forest fire, one that matched her own, flame for flame, it was *she* that wanted to go back for more.

Until she heard Mina saying, 'Get a room.'

Shock snapped her back into the present, back into the VIP room, where a few other guests had seen them and broken into gentle giggles and one wolf whistle.

'Careful, Mina,' Leo warned his ex-fiancée over Helena's shoulder, desire morphing into disdain. 'Your jealousy is showing.'

'Me?' Mina practically screeched. 'Jealous of her? You're kidding, right? She was never anything more than a puppy that followed you and your brother around, picking up whatever scraps of attention you dropped on the floor.'

And just like that, Helena was back outside Leo's bedroom, listening to the conversation that had broken her teenage heart. Hurt bloomed beneath the truth of Mina's words. She *had* followed them around, desperate for whatever attention the Liassidis twins would give her.

'Mina,' Leo warned, the tone of his voice enough to raise the hair on the back of Helena's neck.

But it was too late. Helena's memories crashed around her in a red haze, the desire filling her chest replaced with a thick, painful ache. That last Christmas she had spent on the Liassidis island with her parents before everything changed. Before Leo started to treat her like a stranger, before he and Leander began to argue in earnest. Before her father had passed away and her mother had ruined everything.

All of it followed on from that one overheard conversation that had fed painfully into insecurities already burgeoning within her teenage sense of self.

'She's just a child. She's nothing to me.'

Helena clenched her teeth to stop the tremor of tears from creeping onto her tongue, to keep her mouth from wobbling.

'Do you have to dress like that?'

'Do you have to wear that?'

'Do you have to want so much, Helena?'

'You should be able to do this on your own. I can't do everything for you.'

Her mother's voice mixed with the memory and it became louder than a drumbeat. She slipped from Leo's lap, cold and shivery from the stark difference in mood and tone, and looked up at the woman currently glaring at her with such undisguised jealousy it actually hurt to look.

It was clear that Leo's ex-fiancée had her own demons and it wasn't Helena's responsibility to carry them. But she wanted Mina to know. To know that she had heard what Mina had said that day. And perhaps a small, devastated part of her wanted Leo to know too.

'Well,' Helena said to Mina, finding her strength, 'I guess someone *trained me better* in the end. Because even though I'm *just the daughter* of Giorgos's business partner, *I'm* the one wearing a Liassidis ring.'

Mina's eyes flashed in the dark of the nightclub, clearly realising that Helena had overheard her conversation with Leo. It was a petty shot and she shouldn't have said it, but Helena was hitting back at all her childhood hurts any way she could.

Beside her, Leo flinched but Helena didn't pay it heed. 'It takes a really troubled woman to blame a girl of fifteen years old, Mina. And as for Leo. If I remember rightly, you left him. You chose to walk away from him because it looked like he could lose his company. You walked away because you couldn't see his worth. It had nothing to do with me.'

'Nothing to do with you? You and your mother—'

'Enough,' Leo said, standing up, cutting off Mina's words before she could do any more damage. 'He knew, Mina,' he announced with cold disdain. 'Leo knew what kind of woman you were. He might not have realised it at the time, but the moment you left, it was a blessed relief for him.'

His words caused goosebumps to scatter over Helena's skin, beginning the healing of a part of her she had refused to acknowledge. Leo turned and held his hand out to her and she took it, leaving Mina, open-mouthed with shock, watching them as they left the club.

They stepped into the night, emotions so thick between them they were almost visible, like hot breath on a cold winter's night. She could all but feel the fury rolling off Leo in waves.

'Leo?' she asked uncertainly as he pulled her along practically at a jog into the night.

'Not here,' he growled. 'I will not talk about this here,' he went on, his words harsh and final. A car pulled up to take them back to the helipad and Leo was silent all the way back to the villa.

Leo stalked into the villa, wanting to slam doors and punch walls. He hadn't been like this since those first few years after Leander had walked away from everything they'd planned—from the company that they were supposed to take over from their father together. From the *lives* they were supposed to lead together.

And somehow all of it had been made worse by the Haddens and it had just become a jumbled mess in his mind that he'd refused to think on. Only now it seemed that the fates were conspiring against him and finally forcing him to face it all.

He crossed the living area to the wet bar in quick strides, wanting only to feel the burn of the alcohol in his throat rather than the aching hot twist of shame that had sprung the moment he'd realised where he'd heard Helena's words before. *When* he'd heard them.

'Why didn't you tell me?' he demanded, unable to look at her, staring at his white-knuckled grip around the glass.

'Tell you what?' Helena asked from behind him.

He clenched his jaw and turned, pinning her with a stare. He hadn't bothered to turn the lights on when they'd got back, but the gentle glow of the solar-powered garden lights lit the room through the floor-to-ceiling windows, picking out the glittering sequins on her dress and the sparks of defiance in her eyes.

'Why didn't you tell me that you overheard our conversation that day?'

He watched her expression change into something like incredulity. She let out a burst of air that sounded alarmingly like a scoff, but he could still see the pain she was valiantly trying to hide from him.

'What?' he demanded.

'You're angry because I didn't tell you?' she asked.

'Yes,' he slammed back. Knowing that it was a lie. That wasn't why he was angry at all. He was angry because he'd been in the wrong that Christmas Eve. He should never have said those things to Mina about Helena. And he should never have allowed his girlfriend to say such things. But being in the wrong didn't fit the story that he liked to tell himself about what happened back then—that every wrong thing was Leander's fault and that he had been the innocent victim.

'Why on earth would it have been my responsibility to let you know that I'd overheard you and your horrible girlfriend comparing me to a dog?'

Shame was a hard slap across the face that might as well have left red palm prints across his cheek, the fierce blush there was just the same. He braced himself against the sight of the tears welling in her eyes. He deserved every minute of her pain. And that wasn't even the worst thing he'd said.

'I wasn't… I didn't. Ever.' Not the way she'd made it sound.

'A puppy following you around? That was what you said. Those were your words, Leo,' she returned, and he couldn't deny it.

'I was twenty-one years old,' he defended.

'And I was fifteen! I looked up to you!' she cried.

'But I didn't know what to do with that! You looked at me like I hung the damn moon and I didn't know why.'

The confession burst out of his chest from a place he'd never looked at, never wanted to see. Because Leander had turned his back on him only three years before, and he'd still been searching for a reason why. Helena had openly adored him and it had been confusing and painful and joyous all at the same time. He'd relished those moments, he finally allowed himself to remember now. But then, Mina had noticed.

'Our families always joked about us getting married. And I didn't even care that they teased me about your crush. But Mina did. And when she did, I just…needed to keep you at arm's length.'

'Oh, so you treated me like a stranger for my own good?' Helena demanded. 'Do you think that I didn't realise you weren't interested in me in that way?'

'Lena, you were a child,' he said, his stomach twisting. 'I never once—'

'I know that!' she yelled. 'I know that you and Leander saw me like a sister. And yes, I may have had some silly crush—'

'You barely saw us two months out of the year, Helena,' he dismissed.

'Don't do that. Please don't do that,' she all but begged. 'Don't undermine what having you and Leander in my life at that time was like,' she said, and her words struck him hard. Her words conjured the past he had kept hidden behind a locked door because he hadn't wanted to acknowledge what he'd lost—Leander *and* Helena.

Those summers had been endless and idyllic in a way that seemed remarkable now. Lazy days spent out on the Aegean, the sea breeze and sounds of laughter, the seagulls flying overhead and the simplicity of eating fish caught from the back of the boat.

But then he remembered why it was that he and Leander would take Helena with them.

Because her mother had been too busy focusing on her own interests, and her father had been more interested in business. Yes, they'd entertained her in a kind of absentminded way, but while her father had softened Gwen's coldness, both brothers had felt their rejection of her and tried to protect her from that.

'It devastated me, losing your friendship,' Helena said, unaware of the blows that she was landing on his heart. 'Losing what I looked forward to the whole way through the crappy school year at that god-awful boarding school. No, Leo, I didn't have schoolgirl fantasies of kissing in the rain or something stupid like that. I had dreams of coming to the island and playing on the beach. Lighting fires and swimming in the sea with you and Leander. But when you two fought, all that stopped. There was nowhere to hide from the tension between you, and no way to avoid the heated conflict that would come any time you were in a room together. Which meant that there was nowhere to hide from the fact that…the fact that…my parents didn't treat me the way that Cora and Giorgos treated you. Didn't treat me as if…they wanted me there.'

His heart twisted and turned to see her eyes glistening at her confession. He'd always wondered how much she'd been aware of her parents' casual neglect. He'd hoped that he and his brother had countered it in some way, but now he was realising that the consequences of his fight with Leander had stretched beyond his family. Her emotional confession was raw in her eyes, as if admitting their fighting had cost her too. And he hated seeing that in her, the price she'd paid for their mistakes.

'Lena—'

She shook her head, as if trying to navigate around the emotional boulder that must have been far too heavy to bear. And watching her pull herself together was both remarkable and painful at the same time.

'That was why I hoped you and Mina would work out, even though I didn't like her,' Helena pressed on, breath coming harder and quicker. 'No, she didn't make you laugh like Leander did, but she made you smile again after the separation between you, and that was enough for me. You seemed almost happy again.'

Christós. He'd thought he'd hidden his feelings better. He'd had no idea how obvious he'd been. His parents hadn't wanted to speak about the separation widening between their sons, hoping that it would blow over. Leo had told himself he'd hidden the wrenching pain that was threatening to tear him apart at having been severed from the person he'd thought he knew better than himself. The person who had been almost half of himself.

'I really didn't mean to overhear your conversation,' she said apologetically.

He huffed out a painful laugh. He should have been the one apologising.

'What were you doing there anyway?'

Helena bit her lip. 'I wanted to give you your Christmas present.'

He frowned, remembering more of that day than he had before. 'You didn't get me a present that year.' He'd remembered it because…because of the present he'd bought her.

She inhaled a shivery breath and gave him a sad smile. 'I didn't really feel like giving it to you after…'

Leo nodded. 'I can see that,' he admitted roughly. 'What happened to it?' he asked, curious.

She shrugged, sending a ripple of glitter across the sequins. 'I put it in the hiding place.'

The cubbyhole. It was a place where he and Leander used to leave messages or stupid little things in the house on his parents' island. They'd shown it to Helena when she was little, but he hadn't thought about it for ages. He certainly hadn't looked in it since well before that Christmas.

'It's probably still there,' Helena said as she walked past him to gaze out at the nightscape beyond the window.

He shook his head. Presents, painful misunderstandings. He thought of the peony necklace, the one that Helena thought was from Leander. The delight that she'd expressed in that moment, looking up between him and his brother; he remembered it now like a punch to the chest. It was the last time he'd seen her look like that in his presence.

'I'm sorry,' he said, the words shuddering out of him. 'There is no excuse for my behaviour that day or for what I said.'

Helena stared at the small circles of light punching holes into the darkness, illuminating unfamiliar shapes of shrubs and flowers that were beautiful and bright in the day and bleached and alien in the night. Her arms wrapped tightly around her waist, holding herself together, holding the tears back.

She'd never said that out loud. About her parents. Certainly not about the father that she'd hero-worshipped. Not even to Kate, who seemed to understand without her having to explain. But Leo had been there, he knew. And she wasn't sure that she could hide it any more.

But acknowledging it didn't change anything. It didn't stop her still hoping that one day her mother might soften just that little bit more. Like she had at the wedding. Each time she saw a glimpse of it, of the love there, she wanted more, like an addict only given enough to get by. So, was it naïve to keep hoping for something that might never happen?

Was it naïve to let Leo's apology soften the blow of his words that day? Because if she let that happen, if she allowed him to soothe that hurt…then what would be left to keep her feelings in check? What would stop her from—

She shook her head at the thought. The seesaw of emotions from that evening alone were almost enough to knock her out for a week. Seeing Leo at the club, relaxing and talking to Leander's friends—even if it was just for show—it had seemed for a moment that he was almost having fun. Then dancing with him on the dance floor, running into Mina, the kiss…

She hadn't even had time to think about the kiss.

A kiss that was just for show.

It hadn't felt like it was just for show.

She had felt wanted. Desired. Needed.

But hot on the heels of such an argument? She shivered, tiredness and cold creeping up her skin, wrapping around Leo's apology. There was too much past between them, too much hurt.

'You were having a private conversation with your girlfriend, Leo,' she said in response to his apology. 'There's nothing to apologise for. It's not your fault I overestimated my value to you in my imagination,' she said quietly, making it easier for him. For them. Because now, when Leo was more dangerous to her than ever, she had to have done that. *Had* to have overestimated her value.

Leo pulled her back round to face him, a frown marring those startlingly gorgeous features. 'You didn't. You should never think that. You were hugely important to us.'

Then why was it so easy for you to push me away?

Helena couldn't bring herself to ask the painful question. In part, because she didn't want to hear the answer. It was a question that was all too familiar to her, one that had littered her childhood, not about the twin Liassidis brothers but her parents. When her father was too busy to come to piano recitals and ballet performances. When her mother was present, but so much more absent than her father. Each time they'd failed to show up for her making it both worse and easier to bear at the same time. And then Leo had pushed her away and even now, with Kate—

No. She wouldn't let herself think that. Kate was following her dreams and nothing, *nothing*, would make Helena begrudge her that.

'Helena…' Leo tried.

She shrugged him off. 'It's fine. It was a long time ago,' she said, looking down so that he couldn't see how much she lied.

He placed a finger under her chin and lifted it so that her gaze met his. 'It doesn't matter how long ago it was. I hurt you and I'm sorry.'

His words were a balm she didn't know she'd needed and certainly not one she'd expected, shifting old hurts and unfurling old feelings. She bit her lip to stop the emotion from escaping, but when his eyes dropped to her mouth, she remembered.

She remembered *everything* about the kiss in the club. Her heart pounded in her chest, a flush crept up her body inch by startling inch, and all the while he watched her with an intensity that she couldn't hide from.

He was barely touching her. Just one point of contact, the tip of his forefinger, but she felt *him*. The way that he'd taken possession of her, the way that she'd not cared if she took another breath, the way he'd made her feel alive. Her nipples pressed against the inner lining of her dress, and damp heat spread from her core. The way he'd made her feel, the things she wanted him to do, they all crashed together in a want, a desire so strong that it stole her breath.

His gaze flickered between her eyes and her lips as if he were unable to help himself. Her hands gripped her waist to stop herself from reaching out to him. But it didn't make a bit of difference. Because in her mind erotic images flickered against the backs of her eyes like a multicoloured kaleidoscope… Her hands thrust into his hair as he teased her nipples with his tongue. His open mouth against her skin, his hands around her chest, holding her to him as she rose above him, the shift of his legs as he settled in between her thighs...

Her eyes drifted closed against her will, desperate to cling onto the images for just a little longer. A sigh escaped her lips at the same time she imagined her name falling between them. But that's all it must have been her imagination. Because when she opened her eyes Leo released the tentative hold he had on her and took a step back, and the draught of cold air left in his wake was enough to return her sanity to her.

What was she thinking?

She had married Leander. Even if it was a fake marriage, even if it was just so that she could access her inheritance, and even if, for one second, Leo felt just half of what she did, she had just married his brother in front of one hundred and fifty guests and it had been covered by several international news outlets. The press had been filled with stories about their childhood sweetheart marriage. And if there was even a chance they were discovered it would ruin them both.

And even had she not married Leander, this was *Leo*.

Leo, for whom nothing was more important than Liassidis Shipping, including his brother and his ex-fiancée. Leo, who would ensure that nothing, *nothing*, jeopardised the company he had given so much to, certainly not her. Wasn't that precisely why he was doing all of this? To get her shares away from her?

'We should talk about the kiss,' Leo said as if it were the last thing he actually wanted to do.

'There's nothing to talk about,' Helena replied, drawing a line that couldn't be crossed, no matter how much she wanted to. Because, as she looked into his eyes, she saw that he knew it too. It couldn't happen. Nothing could happen between them. 'I'm going to bed. I have an online meeting in the morning.'

Leo saw the resolution in Helena's eyes and didn't like the frustration he felt because of it.

'Helena. It can't happen again,' he ground out, the words burning his mouth as they came out.

'I know. It was just for show. Don't worry. I didn't mistake it for anything else,' she said, her words scratching against his conscience. 'You did what you had to do because we both thought that Mina was going to out us in public. So, no. It won't happen again.'

But that was the problem, wasn't it? He *wanted* it to happen. Needed it like a feral thing in his blood. It was a ferocity that shocked him to his core. He'd never felt like that about a woman before, not even his ex-fiancée. It felt stronger than a craving. An addiction even. Which was what made it so dangerous. A thing that needed to be leashed. Because he knew what was at risk. His company. *Hers*.

It had taken years to crawl out of the damage done to Liassidis Shipping's reputation after the betrayal of a client was made public knowledge. Years of not putting a foot wrong, or stepping once out of line. He'd been the perfect businessman, determined, focused only on his company and his clients. Focused on doing it his way and by himself.

Even if Helena and Leander publicly split and waited

years, Helena would be seen as his brother's wife for ever. And really, there were only a few sins greater. So, no. It didn't matter what he wanted, or what Helena wanted.

It was simply an impossibility.

The realisation felled him. And he wondered whether, if he was able to go back in time, would he do things the same way that evening? Would he kiss her the way he had?

Yes. A million times yes.

The answer was swift, determined, ruthless, and demanded more. But Leo had more control over himself than most and he wouldn't give in to a selfish desire that would burn through the fragile hold both he and Helena had on the situation that Leander had thrust them into.

'It's okay,' she said to him with a brave smile. 'Tonight we drank to new beginnings, remember? So that's what tomorrow will be. A new beginning.'

She was offering them a lifeline. A fresh start without the weight of the past or the intoxication of the kiss between them in the present. And he both wanted it and loathed it, but it was what they both needed if they had any hope of getting what they wanted from the future.

She held his gaze for one more second before turning to leave the room.

Clenching his jaw and unable to watch her go, he turned back to the window, reaching for a glass of whisky that was now an unappealing room temperature. He heard her steps on the marble floor, taking her further and further away from him.

But, before he could let her go, he needed to know one thing.

'They were good times, though. Weren't they?' he asked her before she could completely disappear.

'Yes,' she said after a moment. 'Yes, they were.'

'You had fun?' he pressed. He held his breath.

'No one made me laugh like Leander did,' she admitted, and he waited, knowing there was more, and knowing that he wouldn't like it.

'And no one made me cry like you did.'

With that final, devastating blow to his heart, she left the room.

CHAPTER SEVEN

Focus, Helena ordered herself as she dabbed BB cream under her eyes, trying to cover the dark circles that had formed from too little sleep. A little blusher and a swipe of lip balm had put a little colour back into features paled from tossing and turning all night.

'I was twenty-one...'

'I'm sorry...'

'It can't happen again...'

Leo's words were background music to images of a kiss that was so carnal, so intense she'd woken up damp, exhausted and miserably unsatisfied. And she would stay that way, she reminded herself, because acting on whatever this was between them would ruin them both.

But at least she wouldn't have to worry about it for much longer. The message she'd received from Kate at some ungodly hour of the morning had put an end to that.

Leander has promised to return to Greece on Sunday.

It had taken Helena a moment to realise that what she was feeling wasn't relief but a sense of loss that shocked her to the core. But Leander was who she needed, so she sent Kate back a series of praying hands emojis.

The alarm on her smart watch beeped with a ten-minute warning and she used that time wisely. She'd set up her laptop under the shade of the thatched pool house awning, aware that Leo would be done with his morning swim. She chose to forgo the peaty Greek coffee she loved to have semi-sweet and opted for an espresso, taking it out to the table, where she made sure that the sun wasn't shining on the screen or the camera.

She flicked through the dossier she'd brought with her on Jong Da-Eun, the German-born Korean actress who had recently gained an international following with a part in a major Hollywood blockbuster. But beyond her celebrity, Jong Da-Eun had a history of charitable partnerships proving her more than capable of being a brand ambassador for Incendia.

She had met Jong Da-Eun about a year ago and, discovering that they had both lost family members in a way that had changed their lives irrevocably, they had formed a fast and firm friendship. Now she wanted to make that relationship professional too.

Helena closed her eyes and inhaled the sea-salt air, taking the time to appreciate the moment. She loved this part of her job—finding the right people for the right role, knowing that it would positively impact not only the charity but the people that it could reach, knowing what good it could do. And she *had* to believe that Incendia would continue. She *had* to believe that she would fix it. That all this was not only worth it, but would work.

The sound of the video call interrupted her thoughts and she settled into the chair and hit the accept button.

'Helena! It is so lovely to see you.'

'Likewise, Jong Da-Eun,' Helena replied sincerely.

'Please, Da-Eun is fine,' the actress assured her. *'Kamsahamnida.'*

Da-Eun laughed easily. 'Your accent is getting better.'

'I've been practising,' Helena confided.

'It's paying off. But Helena, we shouldn't be speaking on your honeymoon,' Da-Eun chided. 'Though,' she added, peering at the background behind Helena, 'it looks incredible.'

'It *is* incredible,' Helena replied, allowing the natural excitement of the location to fill her voice, happy to avoid discussion of the actual honeymoon.

They caught up a little on the details of each other's lives. Helena asking about her latest drama series and the male lead she was paired with, and Da-Eun asking about Incendia and the wedding. Helena hated being evasive, hated having to pick and choose her truths, but if she didn't then neither Incendia nor a possible partnership with Jong Da-Eun would even be possible next year.

Helena's chest ached. She desperately wanted Incendia to be a success. She had worked twice as hard as many of her fellow students, volunteering in the charity sector throughout her studies and beyond, for no extra credit. She had developed her skills until they were honed to a fine point, studying business leaders in the sector and beyond, understanding how their minds worked. She *wanted* to be seen as an excellent businesswoman, just like her father. He had been a titan in his industry and paired with Giorgos Liassidis they had been unstoppable. It was a legacy that she'd wanted not just to be a part of, but to be worthy of.

And she *was* good at what she did. But ever since Gregory's theft she had begun to wonder if she did actually manage to make it through the financial review would that finally be enough to appease the yearning in her heart? For more. For belonging. For *love*.

Yanking her thoughts back to the present, Helena wasted no more time. 'You know how much I've wanted you to work with Incendia, but I really believe that this campaign is the right one for you,' she said truthfully.

'So do I,' Da-Eun replied with a smile.

'Wait…what?' Excitement unfurled like a whip within her. 'You're going to do it? You're in?'

Da-Eun laughed. 'That is why I like working with you, Helena. You can be all work one minute and then a ball of excitement the next.'

Helena blushed and tried to apologise.

'No, don't be sorry. It's refreshing,' Da-Eun insisted. 'This is a cause you not only believe in but have personal experience with. It's so much better than these po-faced men who would do absolutely anything just to make money.'

Helena hoped Da-Eun didn't see the way her words had caused her to pale. Didn't realise how close she had come to the truth. Because wasn't that what she was doing? Absolutely anything to get her hands on her inheritance.

No, she assured herself. It wasn't like that. She wasn't doing it to put the money in her back pocket, like Gregory had, or like countless others who took advantage of any loophole they could find. This was different. Yes, she was doing a wrong thing, but it would achieve the right thing in the end for Incendia, and that was all that mattered. She closed down the call with promises to send contracts and set up meetings for when she returned from her honeymoon.

The shares are yours. The money is yours. Your father made silly, outdated stipulations on your inheritance and you're doing what you have to, in order to save a charity you believe in.

A very Kate-sounding no-nonsense response sounded in Helena's head and she let it soothe her doubts. After all, she had just managed to secure Incendia's first international brand ambassador!

Leo hung back from the threshold, watching Helena's video call, struck by how natural she looked. In control. Powerful in an innate way that he hadn't seen before now. It reminded him of watching his father and hers doing a business deal over lunch.

It wasn't arrogance that had given them a near lazy sense of 'ease', but belief. Belief in their skills, belief in their company, and knowledge. Knowledge that they were the best in the business. And, watching Helena now, he was surprised to find himself enjoying that about her too.

And, just like that, he was regretting not having done his research on Incendia. The way she had talked so passionately about it couldn't be faked. Whoever she'd been speaking to knew it, and so did he. But the person

on the call had called it a 'cause'. And although he loved
his company, he had never met anyone in business who
called their company a *cause*.

What was it about what this company did that made
Helena so desperate that she would marry his brother to
access money to cover the financial hole? The questions
that he'd managed to keep at bay until now began to bur-
row through his mind like woodworm, burrowing little
holes into every conversation they'd had before now.

He watched as she wrapped up the conversation, the
sun catching the golden glints in her hair, the oversized
shirt hanging from her shoulders, indolently revealing
the smooth skin he'd spent an alarming number of hours
thinking about. A gentle tan had sun-kissed her skin
with freckles that looked wholesome, even as his body
responded to the near primal passion he had glimpsed
the night before.

It seemed that, despite the warning his brain had
been given, his body still hadn't got the message. All
night he'd been tormented by impressions of a kiss that
was just as real as his erotic dreams had provided. He'd
woken up, his body on fire and full of a tension that
wouldn't quit until Helena and this entire situation was
firmly in his rear-view mirror.

He was about to turn away when Helena got to her
feet and he realised that the shirt, which stopped mid-
way down her long thighs, was all she was wearing.
Whether it was a shirt or a dress, he didn't give a damn.
He would go out of his mind if he spent the next few
days in close proximity to a woman who was his every
fantasy come to life.

He tried to leave again, when his attention was snagged by her cry, 'Yes!' He turned back to find her dancing up and down as if she'd won some great victory.

'Yes, yes, *yes*!' she cried again.

As she punched a button on her mobile, he wondered when he'd last felt like that about a deal or a contract.

Never, he realised with a start.

Gwen's damage had happened too soon after he'd stepped up to take over the helm from his father for him to ever fully trust or feel such pure easy joy or trust in a new deal again.

'Megan, we did it!' he heard Helena cry into the phone. 'Jong Da-Eun is coming on board.'

Even from here he could hear the high-pitched scream of the person Helena had called, especially when Helena had pulled the phone away from her ear to laugh, and he couldn't help but smile at their exuberance.

'Yes, yes, I know. So can you move forward with the contract? Absolutely... No, that won't be necessary, just send it out to the list in the dossier.'

There was a pause and some of the joy dimmed from her features. 'No update? Nothing from the CPS?'

Leo frowned, recognising the acronym for the British Crown Prosecution Service.

It's not failing. It's employee theft.

'Okay... No, that's okay. If you can just chase Dr Matheson for his research proposal, then we can begin to create the fundraising plans.'

And once again his interest was piqued.

What did Incendia do?

Helena raised her gaze and it clashed with his in shock as she discovered him standing on the threshold.

'No, that's it, thanks, Megan,' she replied, without taking her gaze from his. 'Have a great rest of the day.'

She hung up the phone and now he didn't know what to do. Come out onto the deck? He could hardly turn and leave.

And just when had he become so indecisive and weak-willed?

Throwing off the awkwardness, he brazened it out onto the deck.

'Am I right in thinking that congratulations are in order?' he asked, hating the hesitation between them, the wariness heavy in the air awkward and uncomfortable. He'd almost preferred the intense sexual tension to this.

Slowly, she nodded, the smile on her lips pulling to one side. 'Yes,' she said with quiet confidence, unable to quite hide her excitement. 'I've just secured my first brand ambassador and she's going to be great.'

'Then that *does* deserve congratulations. We should celebrate,' he announced before frowning. 'Or do we have another social event to attend?' he asked with distinct displeasure.

'Celebrate?' Helena asked, as if confused.

'You know, celebrate. Do something special to mark the success,' he offered at about the same time as he realised that it was something she usually did with his brother. 'Unless you want to wait for Leander?' he asked, wondering why that thought filled him with a strange kind of resentment.

'Well, I suppose I could. Kate messaged. Leander's coming back on Sunday.'

Her words had the same impact as a stone thrown into a lake.

'*This* Sunday?' Leo asked, unable to hide his surprise.

'Why? Is something wrong with that?' Helena asked, picking up on his shock.

'No, I just…hope that Kate got him to sign in blood. I'm about done with this whole affair,' he dismissed, despite the bitter taste in his mouth.

Only to see Helena's expression morph into hurt.

'You're not the only one,' Helena grumbled as she made her way past him.

'Wait,' he said, reaching out to clasp her by the arm.

Everything stopped. His heart, her steps.

Slowly, she looked down at his hand, where his fingers had wrapped around her bicep, and he released her immediately. He'd done it without thinking, but the tremors rippling through the air and across his skin warned him it had been a mistake.

'I'm sorry,' he said. For the snarky comment, for grasping her arm. 'I'm…' he took a shaky inhale '…I'm trying. I'm not used to…' he pressed his lips together '…modifying my behaviour. Having to, or even wanting to. Usually, people just do what I say and don't really ask questions,' he admitted hesitantly.

Or talked back, Helena guessed. Because Leo seemed to be talking only about professional interactions. The confession pulled at her heartstrings as she began to see, really see, how the separation between the two brothers had impacted *him*. But even what he had just said seemed much more like the old Leo than the still aloof Leo she had met on her wedding day.

'So,' he tried again. 'Leander's coming back on Sunday. But it's Thursday today and I feel like we should celebrate sooner than that.'

Helena could see that he was trying. That it was an effort for him, but he was doing it for her. And even just the glimpse of what he could be like when he wasn't so angry and rooted in the past made her want to pull him out fully into the light.

'You know…' she said hesitantly. 'I saw that Leander left his prized convertible here in the garage,' she went on, remembering how much Leo had loved to drive. To be in control, but also to be *free* in that control. 'It would almost be a crime not to take it out for a spin on such a beautiful day.'

'Now that, Helena, is an excellent plan,' Leo replied, with a spark in his eyes that she hadn't seen for years.

As Leo manoeuvred the car along the coastal road leading away from the Mani Peninsula and upwards, Helena couldn't help but smile. The powerful car practically purred under his command.

The wind roaring in her ears and whipping at her hair meant that conversation was almost blissfully impossible and she was surprised by how content she was to simply be there in the moment, the sun falling on her shoulders and the stunning coastline a picture of intense blues, startling yellows and rich greens.

This was the most relaxed she had seen Leo since he

had burst back into her life and she was glad of it. As he changed gear, the convertible leapt forward, restrained by his control but eager to show its power.

In tan trousers and a white linen shirt, rolled up to his forearms, he looked every inch the powerful Greek billionaire with the world at his feet and Helena revelled in being beside him. His eyes firmly on the road, his eyes hidden behind a pair of sunglasses, she watched his lips curve into a smile hooked at one side.

'What?' she couldn't help but ask.

'That,' he replied, nodding towards the downward trajectory of the road, at the end of which was a small fishing village. 'Are you hungry yet?' he asked.

Oh, yes. She was very hungry. Just not for what he was able to offer her.

Half an hour later, they were sitting under a blue and white fluttering awning, protecting them from the fierce heat of the sun. The table was one of only about six on the small terrace of the main, and quite possibly only, restaurant in the small village stuck like a barnacle to the side of the coast.

'Are you sure this is how you want to celebrate?' Leo asked, as if he wasn't sure it was enough.

'Yes!' she insisted with genuine sincerity. 'Because honestly, if I have to smile at another reporter, or give another red-carpet interview, I think I might actually murder someone.'

'Well, if it's my brother, then I'll happily help,' Leo replied with a humour that was usually absent when talking about Leander. She ignored the slip, all the while hoping for more. Because she would love nothing more than to help the two brothers find their way back to some semblance of a relationship. Somehow.

The waiter arrived to pour their wine, promising that the food would be with them shortly. They had ordered a fish platter and side of fresh salads, pitta and the hummus she had been lusting after the moment she'd seen another couple dining in the late afternoon sun indulging in the chickpea dip.

'To your new brand ambassador,' Leo toasted.

Helena clinked her glass to his and took a sip of the cool white wine that instantly burst with tart, delicious freshness on her tongue.

'And can I ask what she will be branding for you?' Leo enquired.

Helena swallowed, the wine going down the wrong way and causing her to cough.

Apologising and spluttering, she didn't know why she was reluctant for him to know, even though she was aware that she'd been keeping it from him.

'It's a medical charity,' she started.

Leo's head cocked to one side in curiosity.

'For heart conditions, mainly. But it's one of the only charities supporting the families of people with—'

'Brugada,' Leo correctly concluded.

She clenched her jaw, surprised that Leo had realised, had even *known* the name of the disease that had killed her father. She was touched—moved. They hadn't really been talking that much back then.

Shock rippled through Leo's body with a shiver that raised the hairs on his arms and neck. Brugada syndrome was what had caused Michael Hadden's heart to stop one night in his sleep and never start again. There were rarely any symptoms of the genetic disorder that caused irregular heart rhythms that were often catastrophic if left undiagnosed.

Malákas.

'I didn't know,' he confessed.

'Why should you?' she asked defiantly.

'Because if I had I would never have offered such a low price for the shares. *Christós*, Helena.' Leo's conscience sucker-punched him in the gut so hard he was winded.

'Don't do that,' she commanded. 'I made my choice that day. I knew what I was doing,' she whispered angrily.

'But *I* didn't,' he fired back.

Helena let out a cynical laugh. 'Whether you like it or not, I *made it* as a businesswoman. If you change your mind because you feel sorry for me, you're undermining me and patronising me. On the day we're supposedly celebrating me.'

Realisation dawned in his gaze and he started to shake his head in denial, but stopped as he fully understood what she was saying.

'That wasn't my intention.'

'But it was what you were doing,' she pointed out gently.

'It's not a good deal for you,' he said again.

'Then maybe, in the future, you'll think twice about the deals you offer,' she said, leaning back into the chair, clearly aware that she'd made her point.

He'd been so hell-bent on getting all the shares in Liassidis Shipping that he hadn't even bothered to do his own research. Research he was usually absolutely meticulous about. He didn't like it, the effect she seemed to be having on him. The way he was behaving out of character. But he also didn't like the discord between them. Not after how much he'd enjoyed the peace.

'How did it come about? You and Incendia,' he asked both carefully and curiously.

She could have sniped back at him, he certainly deserved it, but he sensed that she wanted it too, the fragile truce between them.

'After my father passed away, Mum was…pretty difficult to be around.'

Helena had always found it difficult to talk about Gwen. It was as if it were a betrayal to reveal some weakness in her mother's character. Especially to a man who had been so devastatingly impacted by her already. But was grief really a weakness? It affected everyone in such different ways and none that could be predicted until it was felt, experienced.

'At first, Mum was determined to continue on as if nothing had happened. Yes, her husband was gone, but she could cope with that as long as everything else remained the same. And she did that first by trying to carry on with his work.'

Which had been disastrous.

'I…knew that she had made a mistake that had cost Liassidis Shipping greatly, but…' she trailed off, shaking her head '…I didn't know that she'd gone expressly against your wishes, or those of the board. I didn't know that at all. I just thought she'd made a mistake and that you'd...'

'Exiled her?' Leo asked, his eyes lit with a strange mixture of understanding and lingering resentment.

Helena pressed her lips together and nodded guiltily. She understood a lot more now than she had then, as to how damaging that would have been for his company. How it would have felt to have his decisions questioned like that, and to have been so publicly defied. In a way, wasn't that what Gregory had done by stealing such an obscene amount of money from Incendia on her watch?

'We shouldn't have let it happen,' Leo said of himself and his father.

'No one expected her to throw herself into it to that extent,' she admitted. 'But I think it was because... Well, I think because if she could keep everything the same, then nothing had happened. She hadn't lost the man she loved. She wasn't drowning in her own grief. If she was busy, if she was doing something, then she didn't have to think about it. The only problem was...'

'That if she wasn't managing her own grief, she wasn't managing yours either,' Leo concluded correctly again.

Helena nodded. It was strange how much he seemed to understand her without her having to explain. It was familiar, and it both soothed and hurt at the same time.

'My grief was a reminder of things she didn't want to acknowledge. And it made an already difficult relationship painfully strained. One of the teachers at my boarding school referred me to Incendia and it was there that

I got some support for myself, rather than having to neglect my feelings in order to try to protect my mother's. Their help was a godsend.'

But when grief had entwined with the loss of the Liassidises from her life—the anchor that had seemed to hold her little family together—it had felt as if everything had slipped through her fingers. After her mother had failed to navigate her own grief with her husband's work, she had returned to England and thrown out everything that had ever belonged to him. She had put the house in Mayfair on the market without even telling Helena and although it had never really felt like a home it had still been a devastating blow.

Helena had clung to Kate in those early months, and even Leander. But the people she'd missed so terribly, her father and...and Leo, she forced herself to admit, were gone.

'I worked with one of their counsellors, and then began volunteering when I had started to find my feet again. Knowing first-hand how important their work and the funding they raised for such specific research was—the kind that big pharma doesn't have any interest in because the conditions are so specialised there is little financial incentive—just made my work there more important.'

Leo was listening intently, impressed beyond belief at the kind of strength it must have taken to work at a charity where every day she must be reminded of the loss of her father.

'So, after my A-levels, I went to study business management at Cambridge Judge Business School.'

'That's incredible,' he said.

'You sound surprised,' she accused.

'Not in the least.' And he wasn't. Because he had always known, really, that whatever she put her mind to, she could achieve.

'I did my master's there too. Did a few years in the sector, worked as a consultant across a few startups. I won a few awards,' she admitted, as if it were something to be shy about rather than proud, and Leo was back to cursing the mother who had taught her daughter to expect so little.

'And when Incendia approached me about the CEO's position it was… It was a dream come true.'

Leo wondered whether she realised it—how passionate she sounded when talking about Incendia. Helena shone the moment she talked of it, her eyes bright and powerful, the flush on her cheeks nothing to do with anger, or sexual tension. Just joy and inner pride that made her more beautiful than he'd ever seen her.

His conscience twisted painfully in his chest as he realised not only how much he'd missed, but the active part he'd played in her isolation during such a painful and grief-stricken time. He knew then that no apology could cover his behaviour. But he found himself wanting to explain, to justify.

'I had no idea. About Gwen. About…'

Helena bit her lip, but he pressed on.

'About how difficult that time must have been for you.'

'I don't know how you could have. You were too busy trying to save a company my mother nearly destroyed.'

He nodded. 'It's no excuse, but that was a really hard time. Dad had just stepped down from the day-to-day running of the company, and I was working flat-out.'

Mina had broken off their engagement and he hadn't even had time to work through that. He'd been pulling nineteen-hour working days to retain the few clients that had stayed, to keep the workforce on so that when they did get new clients they could fulfil the work orders. He'd refused help from his father, because to accept it would admit that he was failing, and he wouldn't even let himself think about asking for help from the brother who had all but disappeared from his life.

'I wanted to prove myself. I shouldn't have taken it out on Gwen, I know that. Even though I'd told her not to do it, to engage that client, I think that Gwen saw me as a child, an upstart and that she knew better.'

'A little like how you see me?' Helena asked, her tone light, but something serious in her gaze.

And he realised then how truthful that statement was. He felt the sting acutely.

'A little. Yes,' he admitted. 'I still think that you're playing a very dangerous game in trying to plug the charity's financial hole yourself, I won't lie to you. But I understand why you're doing it. And, ultimately, it's your choice as CEO.'

She nodded, but didn't look convinced.

'What is it?' he asked.

'I... What if...?'

He waited. Whatever her fear was here, it was important to her and he couldn't rush it.

She looked down at the table. 'What if it's not enough?'

The desperation in her tone cut him to the quick.

'For who?' he asked.

'The board. My mother.'

The latter was a near whisper that broke what little was left of a very cold, hard heart.

'It needs to be enough for *you*, Helena. No one else.'

Leo knew that better than anyone, because he'd learned it the hard way.

CHAPTER EIGHT

WRAPPED IN A TOWEL, wet hair piled into a messy bun on top of her head, Helena looked tiredly at the dress she was supposed to wear to the lunch Leander had arranged for them at a trendy restaurant that also just happened to be owned by a potential client for his company.

Helena hadn't for a second begrudged Leander using these opportunities to drum up prospective business, at least…not until he had disappeared and left Leo and her in this mess.

She let the printed silk of the dress slip through her fingers as she wondered what would have happened if Leander had stayed. What if she had arrived at the church to find him rather than Leo waiting for her at the top of the aisle?

Yes, everything would have been easier. She and Leander would have smiled and pretended to be the perfect couple. Kissing Leander would have felt silly and stupid, and not far off what it would have felt like to kiss Kate!

But kissing Leo…

Goosebumps pebbled the skin on her forearms.

It can't happen again.

She forced away the throb of desire that undulated

through her body like a wave against the shore. Three days. She just had to get through three more days. As long as they kept to the schedule, she'd be able to make it.

She'd won a huge victory with Jong Da-Eun and Leo had wanted to celebrate that. Yesterday had been wonderful, she admitted to herself. Seeing Leo like that again, talking to him like she once had. He'd been impressed by her, she'd seen it. And that meant more to her than he'd ever know. So much so that she'd confessed her secret doubts—that saving Incendia wouldn't be enough. To make up for the board's doubts in her, her mother's rejection.

He'd told her that it needed to be enough for her, but she couldn't help but feel that nothing she did would fill the hole created by her mother's mental absence and the loss of her father.

Helena shook off the sad thought. What point was it yearning after things that could never be?

Throwing on a pair of loose trousers and a short shirt-top, she went to have breakfast, to find Leo wheeling a cabin bag into the living space.

He was leaving? Now?

'What—' She stopped herself midsentence because she didn't even know what to say. She'd thought that yesterday had brought them closer. At least to a point of understanding. And now he was leaving?

Leo looked up and must have seen the shock pass over her face.

'What's wrong?' he asked, concern stark on his features.

'Why do you have that?'

He looked down, said, 'Oh…' and grimaced.

'Look, if you have to leave—' Helena said, trying to sound nonchalant rather than panic stricken.

'Leave? Why would I leave?' he replied, confused.

'You have a packed case!'

'Yes,' he answered as if she were missing something.

'Why?' she nearly cried.

He smiled then and the sight was so at odds with the entire exchange she wanted to throw something at him.

Oh, this man!

'We're going on a trip,' he announced.

'What trip? We're having lunch at Thentroliváno.'

'*Leander* wanted to have lunch at Thentroliváno, but us? Not so much.'

'We don't?' Helena asked, feeling, against all odds, the tug of Leo's good humour working on her.

'Nope,' he said, shaking his head. 'We do not.'

'So, what is it that *we* want to do today?' she asked, playing along.

'We are going on a boat trip,' Leo announced with an uncharacteristic flourish. 'So go pack a bag,' he commanded.

Helena's mind completely blanked. 'What am I packing for?'

'Swimming, sun, sea and an overnight stay.'

'O-overnight?' Helena stuttered, never once having suffered from the affliction before in her life.

Leo looked away, hoping that Helena didn't see his body's reaction to her simple question.

'Yes, just a change of clothes,' he confirmed as he fiddled unnecessarily with the handle of the case.

Gamóto, he was behaving like a schoolboy.

He glanced up at Helena, who was staring at him, an unfathomable look on her features. He paused, fearing that he'd done the wrong thing, that he'd made a terrible mistake. All he'd wanted to do was to throw Leander's damn agenda out of the window. They'd been playing by the rules of a games master who wasn't even here. And if they only had three days left, then Leo didn't want to waste them doing things that would only benefit his brother.

Yesterday had been a breath of fresh air for him and he was surprised to find he wanted more. It had nothing to do with the fierce arousal which was banked, as much as was humanly possible, by what couldn't be. He had enjoyed spending time with her. Talking to her. Hearing about her life. And, masochist that he was, he wanted more. If this was all they could have, he would take it *all*.

'Why a boat trip?' Helena asked.

'Because whenever you visited the island it was the first thing you'd ask to do. You'd run straight up to us and demand to know when we were going to take you out onto the water. We used to call you—'

'*Delfíni.* You used to call me dolphin.'

Leo nodded, his lips curving into a smile against his will. '*Naí.*'

Helena smiled. It started off small and slow, but grew until he felt it in his heart. There were many things that he could never give to Helena or be to her. But this? This he could do.

'Go pack. We leave in ten minutes.'

The look of excitement that lit her features stopped his breath. Eagerness, joy, a flush that was so damn innocent he nearly choked.

She spun on her heel and ran off to her room, giving him a brief respite from the impact of her presence, and time to calm his body's innate response to her.

And then, with startling clarity, he realised just what kind of hell he'd let himself in for over the next twenty-four hours.

The driver let them out at the large marina where the yacht Leo had organised last night waited for them. It wasn't presently on the market, but the owner was a friend and Leo had paid an exorbitant price to have the yacht's staff sail through the night to have it here on time. And while he'd seen pictures of it, knew its reputation, even Leo couldn't help but be impressed by the thirty-three-metre-long yacht.

Helena drew up beside him and stared, eyes wide and mouth open.

'Boat trip.' The words fell from her lips.

'Mmm?'

'You said boat trip. *That's* not a boat,' Helena said, the awe in her voice making him smile, giving him exactly what he'd wanted when he'd first had the idea.

As if in a daze, Helena drifted towards the yacht, where a uniformed staff member waited at the plank with a smile on their face.

'Mr and Mrs Liassidis? Congratulations on your recent wedding.'

Of course, Leo had told his friend that it was a wedding gift for Leander and his new bride. But he'd forgotten what a nuisance it would be having to keep up the pretence in such close quarters. And he'd wanted this to be a true escape for Helena. A chance for her to just be herself. As he hastily looked for a way round it, Helena let herself be guided onto the yacht.

As directed, he left their bags by the gangplank and followed Helena for a basic tour of the beautiful yacht. Split over three levels, the lower, main and upper deck, the yacht could comfortably house eleven guests along with the five crew members serving on their trip. There was a Jacuzzi on the back end of the main deck and a dining area on the upper deck.

'Your bags have been taken to the master suite on the main deck, but we'd first like to welcome you with a glass of champagne,' the staff member offered.

Helena's eagerness was immediate and infectious, and Leo smiled, enjoying the excitement rolling off her in waves. He gestured for them to lead the way towards the glorious view from the back of the upper deck. The Captain joined them for a toast, congratulating them on their nuptials, and then returned to the cabin, where she piloted them out of the marina and into the Mediterranean.

One by one, the staff members retreated unobtrusively, leaving them alone on the deck. Helena leant against the rail, the wind playing with the strands of hair that had come loose from where it was held back.

He wanted to see it down, he wanted to run his fingers through it, grip it in his fist as he…

Maláka.

He needed to have better control over himself than this. Much better.

'How long do we have?' she asked, without turning to look at him.

He wanted to say as long as she wanted, he wanted to give that to her. But he couldn't.

'We'll return to the marina tomorrow afternoon. But if you want to return earlier—'

'No,' she said, interrupting him. 'No,' she repeated, as if wanting to hold on to this moment as much as he did.

He nodded, and even though she didn't see it, he sensed she knew in that strange shared understanding that existed between people who had spent so long together it didn't matter how many years had passed since they'd seen each other.

Needing to break the moment, he excused himself, heading off to speak to the Captain about the arrangements for that evening.

Helena gazed longingly at the horizon for just one more minute. It was perfect. There was nothing marring the clean sliver of sea beneath the weight of a sky so blue it almost hurt to look at it. She had only ever felt this kind of serenity looking out at the sea. Maybe Leo and Leander had been right, maybe in a past life she had been a dolphin, content to swim the oceans.

She laughed, knowing that if she'd said as much to Kate, the veterinarian would have reeled off facts and figures about their lifestyle and personality, and the pods they swam in. Kate would have been in her pod, Helena decided. And Leander, of course. But might there be space for Leo?

And there, looking out at the clash of deep oceanic blue and light denim sky, she inhaled deeply, easily, for the first time in what felt like months. Despite her ever-constant awareness of Leo, here, out on the Mediterranean Sea, at least there were no reporters. There were no staff members, utterly ignorant of the perilous state of the charity, no terrified board members looking to her to save them. Nothing to fix, and nothing to prove to anyone. She hadn't realised how exhausting that had been for her. But here, just like it had been when she was younger, was refuge given to her by Leo Liassidis.

The sun had shifted and was no longer so harsh on her skin. It felt warmer, softer, almost as if it had known that she'd needed comfort rather than ferocity. She heard Leo's steps on the wooden deck behind her.

'What has you sighing like that?' he asked, and she sent her smile out to the sea.

'The realisation that I needed this,' she lied. Because the truth was, it was the realisation that *he'd* known she'd needed this that had caused her heart to turn.

'It's so peaceful out here,' she observed.

'It wasn't like that when Leander and I used to take you out in the boat when you were younger.'

'No,' Helena replied with a laugh. 'No, it was not.'

She would shriek with delight as they guided their speedboat into a crashing wave, scream as the boat jerked and dipped beneath her, loving the salt on her

tongue and the gleam of pure delight in the brothers'
eyes, and cry out for more.

'You were the only ones to do that. Take me out on
the sea,' she confessed, remembering that her parents
would have rather spent time with Giorgos and Cora
than the child they barely saw through the school year.
'I don't think I ever thanked you for it,' she said, frowning, trying to remember.

'You never have to thank me for that,' he replied.

Helena turned to look at him as he came to stand beside her at the rail. Her heart stopped for a beat. He was
utterly devastating. The close-cut beard against his jaw,
dark and inviting. A pair of sunglasses, hiding his gaze,
his emotions from her. His cream linen shirt was open
at the neck, just enough to tantalise with the dusting of
chest hair she'd not seen on him as a younger man. This
Leo was even more *male* to her. Age had honed his features to perfection and it was hard to ignore the impact
he was having on her.

'But this is wonderful,' she said, forcing a bright
smile to her lips as she looked back to the sea. She
closed her eyes and inhaled slowly. 'I think it's the first
time since discovering the theft of the money that I've
actually just taken a breath.'

Leo's heart went out to her. He could see what a struggle
it was for her, not just because of how much the company meant to her, but because she was a young businesswoman who wanted to prove herself so much that
she'd gone to such extreme lengths. Lengths that were
dangerous, both financially and emotionally.

Surely it would have been much simpler just to borrow the money? Or was he just looking for something, anything, that would have removed the barrier of her wedding to his brother?

'Why did you ask Leander to do this for you?' he asked, struggling anew with the resentment he felt about this entire situation. 'Did he not offer to lend you the money?'

'Of course he offered to lend me the money,' she explained. 'But I *have* the money. It's *my* money. I just... don't have it *yet*.'

Before him was a woman who had to fix things herself. Who didn't want to rely on someone else, who had learned from her father's absence and her mother's neglect that she could only rely on herself. Didn't he know that for himself? But why, when he thought of Helena being like that—like him—did it feel like a punch to the chest? To the *heart*?

'But as to why Leander,' she went on, interrupting his thoughts. 'Because I trust him.'

Leo couldn't help but scoff. 'Trust? Leander?' he demanded, his tone harsh, his instinctive reaction to his brother's betrayal near primal.

'Yes. Trust. I knew that he would be discreet and I knew that he would be there for me when I needed him.'

'That's just wishful thinking. As evidenced by the fact that he's *not* here when you need him,' Leo replied hotly.

But Helena shook her head. 'I know him. I know that whatever it is that came up, whatever it was that he needed space for...it was something incredibly important.'

Leo shook his head, a bitter sneer across his face. 'Leander is selfish. He will always put himself first, make choices that benefit him most, without any compunction or thought for anyone other than himself.'

'That's not true,' Helena replied gently. 'It's just what you want to see in him.'

Helena's open expression and flat denial floored him.

Hot anger, old, dark and thick, something *nasty*, built in him. He'd been softening towards his brother. He'd felt it. Not because of anything he'd done, but because he'd seen how others saw Leander. Right up until just then, when Helena had said that she trusted him. Because Leander had lied to him. Made Leo believe that his brother wanted what he wanted.

Right up until the moment when his father had asked the question, Leo had thought he'd known how his life would be. What it would look like, how it would go. Throughout their teenage years they'd developed a way of thinking that completed each other, balanced each other. Applying that to a business context for their family company would have made them unstoppable. But, beyond that, Leo had believed that they wanted the same things. He'd believed that he'd had companionship, trust, *safety* with his brother. It had been them against the world.

'I want to take the money.'

That was what had been more important to Leander than *he* had been.

The shock, the pain, at discovering that everything he'd thought about his brother had been wrong was devastating to him. It had shaken the foundations of what he believed in, and the only way he had been able to survive it had been to cut Leander from his life. To cauterise the wound with abject denial.

He had taken the tattered ruins of his plans for Liassidis Shipping—the only thing he'd had left after Mina had abandoned him—and forged a path ahead alone. Until he'd eventually forgotten that there was a time when he had shared everything with his brother, and instead now shared nothing with anyone.

'Leander,' he told her hotly, as if he could convince her as much as himself, 'would, and *did*, sell out his own brother for his own selfish whims.'

'In the last ten years, Leander has made time for me to celebrate the wins and commiserate the losses. He's been there to take me out for dinner, or dancing or whatever, because he knows that's something that I need. He has given me so much and, in return, all he got is a forced fake marriage.'

Leo clenched his jaw against the picture she was painting of his brother. Trying to cling to his anger instead of the memories of the times that Leander had tried to reach out to him.

'He was there even when I tried to avoid him because of how embarrassed I was over what happened with Liassidis Shipping and my mother,' Helena said, looking at her hands.

'That's because he didn't have to clean up the mess,' he bit out without thinking. But the moment he saw Helena pale, he regretted it instantly.

'That's because he valued my friendship. So please

don't undermine my relationship with your brother just because you don't have one.'

Her words sliced clean and deep.

'It's not like that,' he dismissed instead.

'You could probably say that to anyone else, but I know what you two were like before your father offered you the choice of inheritance between the family business or a financial lump sum.' Her gaze on him was steady and knowing. 'I know how close you were, how sometimes you were so similar only your parents could tell you apart. That kind of connection doesn't just disappear.'

But she was wrong. He admired that Helena was someone who could grow up with parents like hers and still hope for more. Still reach for, *want*, that familial connection. But he couldn't.

No. From that first moment, from the *second* that Leander had chosen to walk away, Leo had drawn a line. A *hard* line between them. He hadn't wanted to speak to, see or hear from the person who had once been half of him. Leander had come home occasionally so he'd been unable to avoid him completely, but five years ago even those sporadic visits had stopped and Leo had refused all contact since then.

That was how he worked, that was what worked for him. That stubborn determination was how he survived.

Yet still Helena pressed on, unaware of his thoughts. 'But I also know that Leander would have been miserable if he'd worked with you at Liassidis Shipping. And I'm pretty sure that you know it too.'

Everything in him wanted to deny her words. Refute them with all his might.

'What I know is that my brother gave me absolutely no warning. The coward let me think that he was going to come with me and then took the money and ran.'

'What do you think would have happened if he'd joined the family company with you?' Helena asked. And his mind went utterly blank. 'Would you have had help? Would you have had someone to talk to? To share your burdens and your fears?' she asked.

Yes, he answered mentally. *Yes*, to each and every one of those questions.

As if she'd read his response in his face, she nodded. 'But all those things are about Leander helping you, not Leander making his own life a success, doing the things that make *him* happy. Believe it or not, but your brother's purpose is not to make *your* life easier.'

He wanted to be outraged. He wanted to be furious. But he couldn't deny what Helena was saying. He couldn't deny the hurt and the shock and the pain that her questions had uncovered. And he couldn't stop his next words from falling from his lips.

'He left me.'

'I know,' Helena replied sadly. And in her, he saw the pain of a daughter who'd lost her father too young and whose mother had barely been present for her.

'But he chose to do that,' Leo insisted, clinging desperately to his resentment, terrified of what it meant if he didn't.

'Yes,' Helena agreed. 'He had a choice to go it alone, do it the hard way and make something from nothing…

rather than slowly lose pieces of himself working in an industry he had no interest in, for a company that would have ignored him in favour of you. What choice would you have made?'

He was prevented from answering by the appearance of one of the yacht's staff.

'Mr and Mrs Liassidis? A sunset dinner has been prepared for you on the lower deck.'

Helena wasn't sure that she could eat at that moment, but didn't want to offend the staff, who had created a feast of absolute deliciousness. Laid out on the table that looked out over nothing but sea and sky were what looked like twenty or so plates of different Mediterranean delicacies.

Absently, she ran the little silver peony pendant across the chain at her neck as she took in the prettily set table and the romantic candles illuminating the deck. The sun was beginning to set, casting streaks of pink and ochre across a sky turning a shade darker with almost each breath she took.

She felt Leo's presence behind her, the warmth of his body like a physical touch against her skin. Despite the difficult conversation they'd shared there was no animosity between them, but she could tell that Leo's thoughts were heavy.

That wasn't what she'd wanted or intended. But she could see the pain the separation between the two brothers was causing each of them. If she could do anything for either of the men who had been such important figures in her life, it would be this.

To bring them back together.

Once again, petals had been scattered across the table and the deck itself, but this time, when she looked closer, she realised that they weren't rose petals. The shades of white, violet and red struck her immediately. Peonies. The colours of native Greek peonies.

Helena turned to look behind her as the Captain appeared on the deck with the other staff members.

'We'll be heading to the mainland now. Just call when you want us to return.'

Leo nodded as if he knew that this was going to happen.

Something like alarm rushed through her, not from fear of him, but from the thought of being alone with him out here. She could barely trust herself with people around. As if sensing her concern, he placed a hand on her shoulder, as if to anchor her, to reassure her, but that didn't make it any better.

The Captain looked between them, and Helena forced a smile to her lips. 'Thank you so much for all of this, it looks beautiful. I hope you have a lovely evening.'

Reassured, the Captain nodded and took her crew down to the main deck, where a small speedboat idled, waiting to take them back to the mainland.

'I thought it would be easier not to have to pretend that I was Leander and we were married, so...'

Helena nodded, but was instantly regretful having lost the security that the staff members had provided. The *barrier* they had provided to her wants.

She looked back at the peonies on the floor and her heart hurt.

He remembered. He'd always remembered that they were her favourite flower.

Why did he have to do that? she thought, even as the lump formed in her throat.

'What's wrong?' Leo asked.

Tears pressed against her eyes. She couldn't let them fall, but it was all too much. Every time she wanted to put Leo in a box where she couldn't touch him, he did something like this. He showed her that he was more than the unfeeling, cold, aloof man he pretended to be. Instead, he was a man who wanted her to have some fun, who had celebrated her success, who'd been devastated by his brother's choice, and who still remembered her favourite flower. All of those complexities made it impossible to ignore her feelings for him. Feelings that she should deny, but she didn't want to. Not any more.

As she ran the silver pendant across the chain again Leo's gaze centred on it.

'Thank you,' she whispered.

'For what?' he asked, his voice as low as the last of the sun's rays on the horizon.

'For this,' she replied.

He looked away to the table and took in the petals on the floor.

'No,' she clarified. 'For *this*,' she said, holding the necklace with her fingers and his gaze with her eyes.

The muscle at his jaw flexed as his eyes blazed with golden shards.

'You knew?' he asked. 'All along, you knew it was from me?'

Helena smiled, a little rueful, a little sad. 'Leander said he'd picked it because it was a pretty rose.'

'It's not a rose,' Leo replied almost indignantly.

'I know,' she said, his response almost making her smile. 'It was only you that ever remembered I loved peonies so much.'

'Why didn't you say something?'

'Because at first it was easier for me to pretend and not cause any trouble for you.'

'And then?' he asked, his tone hesitant, as if he almost didn't want to hear the answer but couldn't help himself.

'And then it was easier for me to pretend that it was Leander and not you who had given me such a significant present, when it was so easy for you to cut me from your life.'

The truth sobbed in her chest. She no longer wanted to hide anything from him, to protect him, or herself. If this was all she was going to have with him, if this was all they would ever get, she wanted him to see and know even the most dark and vulnerable parts of her. She wanted to be known by him, completely and utterly.

Only by him. Only ever by him.

'Why did you wear it to the wedding?' he asked. 'Before you knew I was going to be there.'

She looked to the ground. 'Because I wanted something of you that day.'

He lifted her chin with his forefinger, pulling her gaze back to his, the question in his eyes not needing to be spoken.

'Because,' she said, drawing on her courage, 'because it's always been you.'

CHAPTER NINE

NOTHING COULD HAVE undone him more in that moment. Nothing had *ever* undone him more. The naked want he saw in her eyes, the yearning. No one had ever looked at him like that. Not Mina, or any of the other women he'd spent time with.

She had kept his secret—the Christmas gift—at first to protect him and then later to protect herself, and he didn't know what was worse. No one had tried to protect him before. Not his brother, or his ex-fiancée. An ex-fiancée who had not even recognised him when they'd collided in the club. But Helena had. The moment she'd seen him at the top of the aisle, she'd known who he was. She *always* had.

It's always been you.

Deep down, he'd known that. He'd felt it but never wanted to look too hard or too closely at it because he hadn't wanted to lose her too. But her desires were written in her eyes and he wanted, so damn much, to give in to all of them.

'The world just watched you marry my brother,' he said, still desperately clinging to the last remaining barrier between them.

Helena nodded, agreement and understanding shining in the depths of the tears that hadn't yet fallen.

'We can't...' he tried again. Tried to convince himself. Tried to lie. When all he wanted to do was take her into his arms. 'It would ruin us both if it were found out.'

Helena bit her lip, her gaze dropping to the floor as she nodded in a way that twisted his gut. She turned to leave and the sudden wrench in his heart nearly killed him. It sliced clean through every and any objection that he could make, any fear for the future or of the past. He couldn't let her go. He just couldn't.

Leo caught her wrist and pulled her back to him and when she crashed against his chest he held her there, caged within his embrace, half terrified that she'd escape.

His entire body tensed against the shock of her against him, so close that he could feel the beat of her heart against his chest. Neither of them moved, barely breathed even, until she sighed and relaxed against him and he felt a victory like he'd never known.

Her head came to just beneath his chin, and he felt the puff of her breath against his neck. Goosebumps unfurled across his skin at the proximity of her lips to his skin, arousal coming for him hard and fast. His pulse raged in his chest and for a moment all he could hear was the sound of blood rushing through his veins.

His entire being wanted to hold, cling, delve, grip, any part of her he could claim. Possession, not sexual, but primal. He wanted her to be his in every way and it shocked him. Shocked him that he could feel something so animalistic when what he held in his arms was so fragile and precious.

She shifted in his hold and for a horrifying moment he thought she wanted to pull away, but when she settled herself against him more securely, when she seemed to relish the press of her body against his as much as he did, his breath eased.

Tentatively, she leaned into him and pressed her lips against his neck and, *Christós*, he'd never felt anything so pure and so wrenching at the same time. The constant tug, back and forth, suddenly stopped the moment he felt her lips pressed against the column of his neck. Arousal shot through him like an arrow, but he held himself back, fiercely curious to see what Helena wanted to do, content and excited to let her lead.

Her hand came up between them and splayed the shirt open at his neck, releasing a button to give her more skin to caress. His fingers gripped her hip reflexively and she pressed herself against him in response.

When she kissed the top of his chest, her tongue swept out and he nearly jumped out of his skin in desperation to join with her, to meet her, to give her even just a taste of what she was doing to him. But he couldn't move. He was under her spell and helpless to stop her sensual explorations.

'Helena…' he tried, his voice coming out on a croak and momentarily unsure as to whether her name was a plea or a prayer on his tongue. Until he realised. It was a plea. It would always be a plea—because he would never need permission to worship her.

She leaned back, still holding on to him by his shirt,

her lips not even remotely as swollen as he wanted to make them, the flush on her cheeks nowhere near what it would be when they were done. Her large sapphire gaze, open, vulnerable and showing all of her wants, was utterly irresistible.

'Please, Helena,' he all but begged. 'Stop me now.'

Helena dropped her gaze to his chest, her brow just slightly furrowed.

'Is that what you want?' she asked, refusing to meet his gaze.

'Not for the entire world,' he answered with raw honesty.

He watched her response, the slow close of her eyes, the breath caught in a chest pressed against his so that he could feel the slightest movement, the heady fragrance of crushed peonies beneath their feet and the soft scent of *her* reaching up to bewitch him.

'Then no,' she said, opening her eyes and locking her gaze with his. 'I won't stop you. Do what you will.'

Need clashed with the last vestiges of his control, thrashing against the leash of his restraint.

'And what is your will?' he demanded, his voice harsh, but broken by the strength of his want. Needing to hear her desires, needing her to be in this as much as he was.

'My will is that you take me, own me and make me yours so that I will be ruined for any other man to come.'

He searched her eyes, her face for any sign of fear or insincerity, but there was none. She meant what she said. And it was a command that he would follow to his last breath.

'As you wish,' he replied, before claiming her mouth with his. As his tongue thrust between lips opened on a gasp, meeting the push of hers, his fingers flexed and fisted, the silk of her printed dress sliding over skin he needed to touch as much as he needed oxygen.

She moaned into his mouth and his chest nearly burst with need. His hands came up to cup her face and he angled her beneath him, taking full advantage of his height, bearing down on her with all the need and passion he was so desperate to share. Her hands came to his wrists, not to stop him but to keep him there, as she opened herself to him in utter and complete surrender.

'Don't hold back,' she whispered against his lips. 'Please don't hold back,' she begged.

Helena's body was on fire, everything burning for him, from him. She didn't think her heart would ever recover, her pulse, her breath would be ruined for ever by the sheer power of her need for him.

He pulled back from a kiss that was so overwhelming she had to steady herself against his chest. The incessant pulse between her legs, the ache low in her core, the dampness on the silk of her panties, Helena swore he knew it all.

He held her gaze as his hands dropped to her thighs, fisting the silk of her dress in his hands, inch by inch, the sensual glide against her ankles, her calf muscles, her knees and upward to her thighs. She pressed her legs together as he pulled the silk higher and higher, towards her hips, and shivered not from the cool sea air that hit her damp sensitive flesh but from the promise in the dark swirling depths of his eyes.

His fingers gripped the flesh of her backside and slipped beneath the bunched dress, the silk falling over his hands as if hiding the deliciously wicked things he was about to do from the world behind a veil of civility. His palm rounded the curve of her bottom, his thumb playing with the string of her silk thong, pulling it taut against her clitoris, and fire exploded across her skin and ignited a deep need in her soul.

Her head fell back and her mouth opened on a cry as his other hand slipped beneath the front of her panties, one long finger gliding down the centre of her slick folds, slowly back and forth, the palm of his other hand still pressed against her, while his gaze still held hers captive, as if demanding that he see every single expression that he wrought from her.

A sob fell from her lips and desire sparkled like gold shards in his eyes.

'Again,' he commanded.

She frowned, momentarily unsure and distracted by the play of his hands.

'I want to hear the sounds you make,' he whispered harshly into her ear, as if he were as affected by her pleasure as she was.

She didn't know why it was something she struggled with, keeping her arousal silent, quiet as if it were her own.

'Or do you need me to help you with that?' he asked, his gaze ferocious with anticipation, a slash of red across each of his cheeks. 'Oh, Helena,' he said, before he slipped his finger deep into her, melting her entire body in a single stroke. Her head fell back but she was anchored between his hands. 'You have no idea what the sound of you does to me,' he said, and the thought of it, the want to do that to him, for him…

He added another finger and brushed her clitoris with his thumb and she saw stars. His palm pressed against the curve of her bottom, his fingers a caress, a grip, before pressing between her cheeks, the startlingly wicked play sending a shudder across her entire body.

Gasps fell from her lips unbidden, and victory shone in his gaze. Her breath shuddered in and out in time with the movement of his hands, and in her mind's eye she saw them: Leo wringing pleasure from her, holding her in her most intimate, sacred femininity, herself near mindless under his ministrations.

Her breaths came quicker and quicker, the closer he pushed her towards her orgasm. She both feared it and wanted it more than life itself, because never before had she felt such a crescendo of sensation that her body vibrated with it. He was her anchor in the storm that came for her. He was the one that held her, even as he caused that very same storm—and even, she could barely believe it, as he promised more was still yet to come.

Her breath caught as she was hurled towards the precipice, no longer caring what sounds she made, gasps and cries of pleasure, need and want, carried away on the sea air. She was no longer Helena, but want, desire, a need that couldn't be stopped, a force that couldn't be dimmed. And when her orgasm crashed over her she fell against Leo, utterly spent and overcome.

She was vaguely aware that Leo picked her up as if she were delicate and precious and, slowly, he walked them down to the main deck, past the luxurious living area and back towards the master cabin she had yet to see.

He paused on the threshold, as they both took in the suite that had been prepared for a honeymoon. More peony petals littered the floor, candles in hurricane lamps glittered and flickered from the breeze coming through the open window, displaying dusk at its most beautiful. Sea salt played on the air and she knew in that moment she would always associate that smell with Leo. The breeze pulled and pushed at long net curtains that hung from the ceiling, encasing a king-sized bed in filmy romanticism.

And she realised with sudden, stark clarity that this was all they could have together, it was all they would ever get. Leo tightened his hold on her as if he'd had the same thought. She reached up to him then, and this time it was she who wanted to anchor him, to this moment, to what they'd given in to so selfishly. If they could have one thing, just one, it would be this.

'Stay with me?' she asked.

'For as long as I can,' he promised, truth in his words, refusing to shy away from the constraints that were shaping the rest of their lives.

Leo placed Helena gently on the bed, shocked at having discovered that she was the greatest fantasy he'd never known he'd had. How on earth had he got so lucky and so unfortunate at the same time, as the seconds they had left slipped through the cradle of his fingers?

Ruthlessly shoving that thought aside, he slowly began to undo the remaining buttons on his shirt, his gaze never once leaving her. He took in every detail, every line of Helena's body, the way her breath moved her chest, the way that the silk dress hung off her shoulder, exposing a stretch of unmarred, perfect skin he wanted to lave with his tongue.

As he shucked the shirt from his shoulders, Helena came to kneel on the bed, drawing the silky dress from her body and throwing it aside. She was glorious in her thong and nothing else, her eyes on his, hot, urgent and expectant, the restlessness of her arousal all he wanted to ever see her dressed in.

'You're magnificent,' he said. 'And I am undone,' he finished in Greek.

The yearning in her gaze softened and somehow that hit him harder than anything else that they'd shared up until now. He felt his heart trip, a warning sign he could not pay heed to.

He crossed to the bed, flicking open the clasp on his trousers, toeing out of his shoes and there, barefoot and barely dressed, Helena looked at him as if she were starving, and damn if it didn't make him feel like a god.

Kneeling at the edge of the bed, Helena reached for him, her hands landing on the waistband of his trousers, gently batting away his hands, her fingers exploring with no shame or embarrassment, simply pure desire that humbled him.

Slowly, she drew the zip down, each tooth grating on

his exposed, raw and as yet unsatiated desires. Her gaze was on her hands, but he wanted to see her eyes. He reached down and lifted her chin with his forefinger. The sapphire blue of her gaze was clouded with untamed passion.

'You don't have to do that, *agápi mou*,' he said, looking down into features that drew his heart into a quicker rhythm, but when her lips pulled into a line of wicked intent, it stopped altogether.

'I know,' she replied, and slipped the trousers and his boxers from his hips and helped him out of them before tossing them to the side.

Her hands returned to his hips, to gently caress the hard length of his arousal. His cock bucked against her hand as she wrapped her fingers around the length of him. *Malákas*, he was too ready for this. He was about to pull back, when she guided the head of his penis into her mouth and all thoughts disappeared from his mind in a heartbeat.

It was heaven and hell combined. The soft, wet heat of her mouth encompassed him and this time he did pray to every conceivable god in the known universe. He felt such intense pleasure—heightened only by the knowledge that being with her, joining with her would be even more incredible.

Her tongue swiped the head of his penis and he couldn't hold back the growl of pleasure that burst from his chest. Her hands cupped his backside, and she took him so far into her mouth he was unable to prevent the thrust of his hips—a primal response born of a need so powerful he no longer was sure he could control it.

But when she mewled her own desire-drenched response he could have cried out to the heavens. She was going to be the death of him, but it was a death he would welcome with every ounce of his being.

Her cool fingers against his skin were a contrast to the heat of her mouth, darkness and light, fire and ice—everything about them clashed and contrasted, but all he wanted was her. He gently pulled himself back, unable to resist the lure of finally joining with her, and he reached into the nightstand, where he was sure he would find a condom.

Helena's eyes were glazed with heady desire, clearing only a little when she saw what was in his hands.

'I'm…' she started, before clearing her throat and trying again. 'I'm on contraception.' She bit her lip, the first sign of hesitation he'd seen in her since they'd first kissed. 'I don't want anything between us,' she confessed.

His heart jerked again. And he took a moment. This was a line that couldn't be uncrossed. He'd never shared himself like that with another woman. Never. But Helena's request floored him. He wanted to give it proper thought, needed to, because the raging urge of his desire was scaring him enough.

'I can show you my test results,' he offered eventually, seeing the sincerity and want in Helena's face. 'All negative. If you're in any way—'

'I trust you.'

Her words ricocheted through his heart and into his soul. It was the most precious gift he'd ever been given.

* * *

Helena was nervous right until the moment she saw her words land on him. As if they'd settled into his skin, his body, and formed a cord between them, tying them together. A part of her wanted to deny it as much as welcome it—because of what it meant. Of what it would mean for tomorrow and the day after and the day after that. Because they didn't have those days. Not really. They only had this.

As if he'd understood her chain of thought, he came to her, gathered her into his arms and kissed her with a passion that would deny tomorrow—deny the future if he could. He kissed her all the way back until she lay on the bed, surrounded by him, encased in his arms, embraced by his hands and imprisoned not by his body but by his passion. She relished it, because it was not a cage of oppression but bonds of safety and security. She knew that, whatever they shared, he would take care of her, protect her, put her first. He would see her and know her, the deepest truth of her, and that was all she needed, she assured herself, before he nestled between her legs and slowly, exquisitely, entered her, inch by delicious inch.

Her head tipped further back into the mattress as the way he filled her undulated across her entire body. Her hips rose to welcome him further, her chest pressed against his, her fingers wrapped around the forearms braced either side of her head as they joined in a way that made her question where he ended and she began. Her breath filled her chest and she was full...full of him, of her, of them, of joy and passion and fear and future loss, but, above all, love. And love was what pushed her over the edge into the second orgasm that swept her away into bliss.

Helena opened her eyes as the sun stretched its first rays across the line of the sea and cursed herself for having fallen asleep. They only had so much time together and she hadn't wanted to waste a single moment.

She turned in the bed to find Leo on his side, looking down at her, his gaze soft for just a moment before he hid it behind something much more enticing. His hand reached across her stomach, wrapped around her side and pulled her across the bed so that she was nestled into his side. She laughed, unable to help herself, relishing this side of his autocratic nature, relishing his possessiveness.

While it had been unspoken, while they'd not said it out loud, she knew that this was all they would have. This was all it could ever be. Leo wouldn't, and shouldn't, risk the reputation of the company that he had given so much to, that had cost him so much. And really, ensuring Incendia's survival would take all her focus. And if she hid behind these excuses of their day-to-day responsibilities, rather than facing the painful truth that Leo just might not want more than this time, she allowed herself dishonesty. Because if this was the reward, she would take it with both hands. And it would be enough, she told herself. It had to be.

Shoving her thoughts aside, she looked up at the man staring back at her. The close cut of his beard was just a little softer than yesterday, the lure of it so great that she reached up to run the palm of her hand across his jaw.

He indulged her touch, letting her hand drift down the long, thick column of his neck, over the broad curve of his shoulder and across muscular traps and delts that she delighted in. He let her explore his body that morning, her fingers pressing and smoothing over every inch of him, as if she could commit this to memory and live on it for the rest of her life.

He let her lead their erotic dance, as she rolled him onto his back to straddle his hips, finding just the right pace, the right pressure point. She felt as if he might have looked on her with something like awe, but was unwilling and unable to hold on to that thought as yet another orgasm rocked them both into such sweet oblivion.

He gathered her in his arms and took her into the large en suite bathroom. White marble veined with grey and green, gold fittings and a dark wood so rich it hummed with warmth made it feel even more luxurious. He turned on the shower, hand beneath the water until he was happy with the temperature, and when he was, he drew her beneath the spray.

With as much care and attention as he'd shown in their bed, he soaped his hands and ran the suds gently across her skin. Never had anyone shown her such care and consideration. This was touch—not for pleasure, but still pleasureful. It was intimacy, not carnal but still erotic. He didn't say a word the entire time, his dark hair slicked with water, skin slippery with soap, hands roaming all over her body. He was as focused on her as she had been on him earlier, and yet somehow his actions, this, nearly brought a tear to her eye.

In that moment she was the centre of his world and she knew it.

And even if it was just for now, she'd take it.

CHAPTER TEN

'WHERE ARE YOU?' Helena called out from the sun lounger on the main deck.

'I'll be there soon. Just wait.'

But she didn't want to wait, she thought, and nearly laughed at herself. Had he cast some spell? Had they turned back time to when she was an infatuated teenager, desperate to get just one more glimpse of Leo Liassidis? Even though she knew it was more than an infatuation, she told herself that was what it was, what it needed to be. Because she was going to find it so hard to walk away when...

'Ta-da!'

Leo loomed between her and the sun, casting himself and what he was carrying into shadow through her sunglasses. And for a moment it felt like a warning, the cut-out of where he would never be in her life.

She bit her lip, forced a smile to her face, took off her sunglasses and gasped when she saw the tray he was holding.

'You made all this?' she demanded.

'Of course,' he replied, as if outraged that she thought he wasn't up to it.

The platter held bowls of beautiful fruits, yoghurts, nuts and seeds, golden and toasted, flutes filled with mimosas, and even two plates with delicious-looking omelettes.

'Of *course*?' she repeated on a laugh. 'You can cook?' she asked, teasing.

'Is this because I'm Greek or because I'm a man?' he demanded, leaning into one hip and making her laugh even more as his outrage deepened. 'Because I need to know which before I can be offended appropriately.'

'Both?'

A string of Greek curses filled the air and she couldn't help it. She threw her head back and laughed, a deep, stomach shaking, heart resetting laugh that she remembered from her childhood.

'Stop laughing like that,' he mock-complained as if she didn't know how much he enjoyed seeing it.

Over breakfast they talked about what they would do that morning, for lunch, for dinner that evening, as if the spectre of Leander's return didn't hover over their shoulders. As if there would be a hundred tomorrows to come.

Swim, eat, luxuriate. It all seemed so easy and so free. So different to the way that she'd spent the years since she'd last seen him. From the moment her father had passed away, she'd been so focused on working with Incendia, on earning her degree, her master's, on being the best that she could be, hoping, wanting so badly to be someone her father would have been proud of, someone that her mother could…could love.

And somewhere in that, she'd forgotten the girl she had used to be. The one that laughed and played in the sun and the sea. The one who had delighted in the teasing fun offered by the Liassidis twins as much as her father's attention. And it wasn't just she who was learning to relax in this moment.

The Leo she remembered from her childhood unfurled beneath the sun, the smile so far from his lips only a week ago nearly a constant. The heat in his eyes, the promise there, was entirely unfamiliar but utterly thrilling and it left Helena feeling so aware of herself and her sensuality—it was powerful and heady, and terrifyingly addictive.

Leo thrust out an arm to catch Helena around the waist, her skin slippery in the saltwater of the Mediterranean, the swimming costume high on her hips and low on her chest. He'd never forget this as long as he lived.

As he trod water, and ducked to avoid the splash she sent his way, he pulled her against him, his body delighting in the feel of her warmth, her skin, *her*. With the islands in the distance and the sea surrounding them, he racked his brain to find any moment more perfect than this.

He remembered seeing Helena at the bottom of the aisle of the church in her wedding dress. Before she'd seen him, before she'd realised that it wasn't Leander waiting for her, there had been a moment—the length of a heartbeat—when he'd forgotten. Forgotten why he was there, forgotten that she wasn't his fiancée, forgotten the feud with his brother... In truth, he'd nearly forgotten his own name.

She'd had a small smile on her lips, a Mona Lisa

smile, hypnotic, cryptic, but alluring nevertheless, and when she'd looked up he'd thought, for just a second, he'd seen recognition in her eyes, delight, hope...before it had turned to horror.

'Earth to Leo,' she whispered into his ear as she twisted in his embrace, their legs sliding against each other as they navigated buoyancy together. 'Come in, Leo,' she finished, the simmering want in her gaze wicked and playful and everything he'd never thought he'd be lucky enough to ever have.

'Well, your wish *is* my command,' he replied as his fingers found the hemline of her costume at her hip.

She squealed in delight, and wriggled, pushing her body further against his, and curses fell from his lips before he claimed hers with his own.

'This is impractical,' he mock-complained against her lips and once again she undulated against him as his fingers found her clitoris. She moaned against him and no amount of cold water could hold back his erection.

'Dangerous even,' he weakly protested, as her head fell back and he anchored her to him and to the surface. He could watch her for ever. He could pleasure her for the rest of his life and it wouldn't be enough.

'Utterly irresponsible,' he tried again as he teased her orgasm closer and closer.

The flush on her cheeks, the gasps of breath on the air, the way she was utterly lost to her own pleasure was almost enough to make him orgasm himself. Her cries grew higher and higher, more urgent, needing, wanting, and he had to try every single trick himself not to follow her over the edge just from watching her come.

Taut lines across her body melted away as she fell into her orgasm and he held her to him, keeping them afloat in the sea, shocked to his core by the single most erotic experience of his life in which he hadn't even orgasmed himself.

Slowly, he drew them back to the boat, pulling her from the sea and into his arms, all the way back up to the main deck, where he washed the saltwater off their skin with the outside shower and wrapped a satiated and smiling Helena in a fluffy white towel.

He drew her to the sun loungers out on the deck. The soft canvas cushion over the wood was comfortable enough for a long laze beneath the rays of the sun climbing too far, too fast, into the sky.

He sat, drawing her between his legs and laying her back against his chest. He couldn't stop touching her. As if his body knew that time was running out and it was desperately trying to take what it could get. All the feelings, all the scents, all the touches.

'So, Ms Hadden,' he began, unable to bring himself to call her by his name. His *brother's* name. 'Curious minds want to know—what is your five-year plan?' he asked in a mock British accent, as if giving an interview.

Only a part of him was interested in the answer, because the other part just wanted to listen to her talk. Or at least that was what he told himself until she hesitated.

'I know that I'm still quite young, and there's so much I'd want to do with Incendia...'

If she managed to succeed in surviving the end of year financial review. He heard her doubt, he knew of her insecurities. But no matter what passed between them here, or in the future, he knew that she would do it. Knew it with a visceral belief in the woman in his arms.

'But one day, in the not-too-distant future, I'd like a family,' she admitted, scrunching her nose.

His heart stopped. Completely and utterly. The high-pitched whine in his ears was like that of a heart monitor flatlining.

'Children. More than one,' she said, her voice stronger the more she entertained her hopes for the future.

As she painted a picture of the family and the life she wanted one day, he forced his body not to betray the ice-cold hold that had taken him over. He, who had fought with his brother for fourteen years, who had immersed himself in work and business and meetings to fill days that had become increasingly empty the more he tried to protect himself, had never allowed himself to think of a future with a family.

And even if Helena hadn't just 'married' his brother for all the world to see, would he have been able to give her that? The family that she had never had as a child, the kind of love and attention and focus that she deserved and needed? Could a man who had been so ruthless with his twin brother be capable of that kind of love?

'I keep losing you,' Helena complained gently, pulling his attention back to her.

And all he could think was that he'd already lost her.

'What about you, Mr Liassidis? Where do you see yourself in five years' time?' Helena asked, even though she knew that their hearts weren't in the 'game' any more.

'Oh, I think I'll still be sitting at the head of the

boardroom, commanding thousands of employees to do my bidding,' he quipped, even though for Helena it was suddenly not at all funny.

His answer was telling, but it was also calculated, and that was what made it worse.

The moment she had told him she wanted a family she had felt something shift between them. Her first thought was that she shouldn't have told him. Shouldn't have confessed her dreams for the future. And then she got angry. Because it *was* what she wanted and it wasn't unreasonable. She wanted the security and love that offered and she wanted to be able to give all the love she had to another human being. To pour it into them.

It wasn't about getting something in return, getting that love back—the kind that she'd never received from her mother or her father—but she wanted so much to share what was *in* her. And there was so much love to give that it almost hurt.

But Leo's retreat, emotionally if not physically, served as a painful reminder that he was not someone who was safe for her.

No, she didn't think that he was the same Leo who had cut her from his life so easily all those years before. She knew—could see—the toll that the separation with his brother had taken on him, and she understood why he had protected himself by creating that separation. Because, deep down, she believed that Leo was just like her. He was someone who had so much love to give and nowhere, no *one*, to give it to.

But he was also very different to her. Because while she still had hope that things could and would be different, it was as if Leo had drawn a line and moved beyond that hope in order to protect himself.

The thought sobbed painfully in her chest. Because she loved him. She loved him deeply and truly and the thought that he wouldn't accept that love, wouldn't allow himself to feel that love was a visceral pain that rended her heart in two.

Forcefully, she pushed back that hurt. There would be time for that later, when Leo was gone and Leander had returned. For now, with desperate hands, she clung to the thread of the present.

She turned in his arms and craned her head to look up at him.

'Kiss me?' she asked.

Distract me. Make me forget that this ends tomorrow.

The staff returned to the boat late that afternoon, after Leo had reluctantly called them back. The car met them at the marina and their return to the villa on the Mani Peninsula was quiet, but the air was heavy with the unspoken words that lay between them.

Leo wanted to rub at his temples, to relieve the pressure that was building there, but didn't want to show such a sign of weakness in that moment. There was a vulnerability between them and he didn't know if it was his or hers.

All he knew was that there was this pressure filling him with a horrible sense of urgency but no direction to go in. Restlessness moved through his entire body, making him uncomfortable in his own skin.

The car took the coastal road back to the villa, each

turn offering the most incredible view of the Mediterranean, the classic Greek shoreline, rich green foliage covering sandy white rock, stark against a blue that would remind him of Helena's eyes for ever.

But beyond all the beauty he could see through the window, all he could hear was alarm bells. Ones that had been ringing in his ears ever since that afternoon. No. He couldn't lie to himself, not any more. He'd been hearing them ever since he'd seen her that first time in the church, but they'd been getting louder and louder, warning of danger ahead.

The last time he'd felt like this, he'd ignored it. Ignored all the warning signs that his brother was unhappy. That his brother wasn't as one hundred percent committed to their childhood dream as he'd once been.

Oh, he had done a very good job at convincing himself that he'd not known what Leander was going to do. That it had been such a complete shock to him. But could he still continue to do that? Especially now, when it seemed just as important, if not more so, than it had been then.

Back then, he had done absolutely nothing, because he'd needed to be wrong. Because he couldn't have imagined life, or Liassidis Shipping, without his brother—his other half. And here he was again, feeling that same sense of something, someone slipping through his fingers unable to do a damn thing. That same sense of being unable to imagine his future without Helena in it. And that need, that desperation, scared the hell out of him.

The car pulled up outside the entrance to the villa and, not waiting for the driver's help, Helena left the car without sparing Leo a backward glance, her body a study in taut lines and hard angles, as if she were trying with all her might to hold herself together.

Leo remained behind in the car, his jaw clenched and hands fisted. He needed to staunch the fury, the anger he felt…the *fear* that he wrestled with. It was as if they'd condensed an entire lifetime into a week, and only now was he becoming overwhelmed by the emotions. Only now, when he felt her slipping through his fingers.

He got out of the car, spurred on by that thought, slamming the door behind him, uncaring of who heard or what they thought. He stalked into the villa and found her staring out at the view from the living area. His heart raged in his chest, pounding furiously, protesting against the cage of emotions that had it in such a stranglehold.

For a moment they just stayed like that, Helena desperately holding herself together and Leo desperately holding himself back.

'I think you should go.'

Her statement should have shocked him. Should have cut the ground from under his feet. But it didn't. Just like it hadn't that day when Leander took the money and ran. He'd known. All along he'd known. Then. And now.

'We have time,' he bartered as he looked at the clock. It was barely eight in the evening. 'Hours even.'

She shook her head, her eyes still fixed on some invisible point on the horizon. 'It's better if you leave before your brother gets here, don't you think?'

'No, I don't,' he lied.

He couldn't take it any more. Crossing the room, he came to her side and pulled her round to face him. Her arms stayed crossed around her body, in protection, in defiance, and it hit him hard.

She needed that? Protection? Against him?

'We could find a way to make this work.'

The breath left her lips in a puff of air that sounded painfully like derision. And it cut him deep. Shaking her head, she stared at him, incredulous.

'How?' she asked hopelessly. 'How would we make this work? Secret assignations? One weekend here, an evening there, hoping that no one will notice? Or we could wait, I suppose,' she said, her words falling rapidly from her perfect mouth, one after the other. 'Leander and I were going to divorce after a year and a half. What do you think is a respectable time to wait before I start banging the other brother?'

'*Christós*, Helena.' He hated hearing the crass words in her soft English tones.

'Oh, I think we both know that that is the least offensive way to describe what the world would be thinking and what the press would be printing,' Helena replied, hating the words coming out of her mouth.

She was right. He knew she was right, so why was he fighting this?

Hope. That wretched thing that he had tried to sever all those years ago. Hope that things could be different. The same hope that drove almost everything that Helena did in her life. Somehow, it had sprung back into being, yearning for more than he could have.

He reached for her quickly, so that she couldn't refuse him. The kiss was angry, furious, and all the more passionate for its desperation. He prised apart her lips, his tongue possessing her, taunting her, trying to claim her even as she would evade him. But she opened for him, as she always would. Welcomed him, his anger, welcomed it all and gave back her own desperate helplessness in return. She stroked his tongue with hers and he held her even tighter as she slipped through his fingers.

He stalked them back against the window, his body caging hers between him and the glass, his hands moving over her clothes, desperate to find whatever skin he could claim. Her moan of pleasure drove him wild beyond reason and into chaos. But it was the helpless whimper of need, of want, of so much more than he could give that yanked him back from the brink of madness. They broke apart, heaving breaths between them, Leo nearly buckling beneath the agony of losing her.

'Don't do this, Helena. Don't push me away,' he begged, even though he couldn't offer her anything more than this.

'Away from what?' she pleaded. 'I just married your brother!'

'But you didn't,' he ground out through clenched teeth.

'Do you think that matters? The press announced it across the globe, it made headlines in twelve different countries. How on earth could anything between us *ever* happen? You barely survived one Hadden. You wouldn't survive this. Liassidis Shipping wouldn't survive it.'

The look in his eyes was a shock. The fear, even the idea that he might lose everything he'd worked so hard for—she read it as if it were the lines of a book written on his soul.

It was a lightning strike right into her heart, burning

a scar over already damaged tissues. It was the *one* thing she'd never wanted to see. She could have lived with her pain and her loss, telling herself that it was the situation that had come between them. That they had simply been star-crossed lovers. And then she could have still cherished the hope that what they'd shared had meant something, had meant *enough*.

But in that moment she knew. *That* was what she had been trying to protect herself from seeing. That nothing had changed. That she still wasn't enough for him.

The blow to her soul was crushing. It stole the oxygen from her lungs and the ground from beneath her feet. She thought she might have swayed. Leo reached for her, but she batted his hand away.

'Helena—'

'Go. Go now,' she said, shaking her head and turning back out to the view beyond the window, wishing she couldn't see his reflection in the glass and hoping that he couldn't see her tears.

'Helena—'

'No, Leo. It's done.'

Helena held herself together as she watched Leo's head drop. He had given up. It was what she'd expected, what she'd thought all along, but that didn't mean it wasn't a stab to the heart.

Slowly, the shadowy image in the window turned, and she watched Leo Liassidis walk out of her life for the final time.

Helena woke up, not sure why and confused as to where she was. Her eyes ached from crying the night before and it took a while to prise them open. She was still in the living area. The sunrise must have woken her. Sleep had been her drug again and she should know better. She had barely eaten anything since the boat and that was more hours ago than she cared to do the maths on.

But an empty stomach was nothing compared to the agony in her heart. The force she'd needed to use to hold herself back as she'd watched him leave had bruised her chest. Every time she breathed the pain was a reminder of what had happened.

He'd gone. He'd walked away. She wasn't enough. She never had been.

'It needs to be enough for you, Helena.'

Her stomach clenched so viciously she rolled into a ball to protect herself from the hurt. She hated that he was right. Hated that he had been the one to say it. Nothing she did with Incendia would make her mother feel something she couldn't. Her father was gone and would never be able to give her what she needed. She had to be enough for herself, but right now things were too raw and too painful from the loss of Leo for her to be able to consider it properly or even understand what that would look like.

A sound came from somewhere in the villa. The sound that had woken her.

She rolled her shoulders and swallowed. Leander was due back today. Perhaps that was him calling now, she thought, finally recognising the sound that had woken her as her mobile phone. She'd put it on silent when they were on the yacht, not wanting to have her last time with Leo interrupted by the outside world.

A tear escaped as her heart melted in a painful sob.

She couldn't do this, she thought furiously. She wasn't allowed to collapse, she wasn't allowed to cry. She clenched her jaw and pulled herself up from the sofa.

In the shower she scrubbed every inch of her body and washed her hair, turning the water from scalding hot to freezing. Everything she could think of to give her body the jolt she needed to come back to the present. But somehow, despite everything she tried, she knew that she'd let part of herself, her heart, leave with Leo.

Dressed in a simple shirt dress, with her hair in a towel and her phone buzzing *again*, she finally went to retrieve it from beside her bed and gasped.

Thirty missed calls?

Some from unknown numbers, a worrying amount from Megan, despite the fact that it was six a.m. back home.

What the hell was going on?

Just then someone pounded on the door. 'Helena? Are you in there?'

She walked towards the door on slow, jerky feet.

'Is Leo with you?'

She pulled up short, eyes wide, body tense with shock.

'Why is Leander in California, Helena, and who is the blonde with him?' another voice demanded as someone tried to peer through the window.

Helena jumped back and then jumped again when her phone rang in her hand. She answered it without thinking.

'Helena? Are you okay?' Megan's voice asked.

'What's…what's going on?'

'They know, Helena. They know that it was Leo with you, not Leander.'

CHAPTER ELEVEN

LEO LOOKED OUT at the Aegean from the coastal path on his parents' island. He'd taken the helicopter and arrived the night before, forgetting that his parents were away visiting friends in France.

But he was thankful for it. He told himself that he *wanted* to be alone. That after seven days of nothing but Helena it would do him good. He told himself that he didn't care that the place felt empty, that he didn't somehow know that *any* place would feel empty now.

He picked up a rock from the ground and hurled it into the sea, where it was consumed by grey, angry waves. He had woken up after a restless night, tossing and turning, to find the sun clawing its way into a startlingly cold and grey morning. The wind whipped cruelly around the island and pulled and pushed at the trees on his parents' estate.

Lonely. He felt lonely.

That's what happens when you turn yourself into an island. Just like the one you're standing on.

His brother's voice had been getting louder and louder and much more frequent in the last week than it had ever been before. Leo's head hurt from the tug between the past and the present, his brother and Helena.

And that's what happens when you don't fight for what you want, the voice taunted.

Leo growled, turning around, half expecting to see his brother striding towards him from the house, but there was no one there. He wanted to fight, to lash out, to get rid of this feeling in him. The feeling of guilt, of shame, of helplessness, because the voice was right.

He hadn't fought for what he wanted. Because, deep down, all along, he'd known that Leander wasn't happy, hadn't he? He'd pretended not to see it; he'd pretended to be shocked by his choice. Oh, it had still been utterly horrifying to experience—his brother choosing the money over him. But he couldn't lie to himself any more. He couldn't afford to.

What Helena had said about Leander was right. Leander would have been utterly miserable at Liassidis Shipping. He was a risk-taker, a daredevil, who would have been suffocated by the company that involved the more grounded and staid work that Leo relished. Because *he* suited *that*.

And why hadn't he fought it? Why hadn't he tried to face Leander all those years ago? Because, deep down, he couldn't shake the feeling that even if he had fought for his brother to stay, it wouldn't have changed a thing. Because he wasn't enough. So it had been easier to paint Leander as the guilty party. As the one responsible for it all. For Leo to emerge blameless, the martyr who had sacrificed all for the greater good of the company.

A sacrifice he'd made all over again.

Helena.

Just the thought of her was a sucker punch to his gut—enough to make him double over in pain. And in that moment he realised that what he'd felt when Leander had walked away was almost nothing in comparison to the earthshattering loss of Helena.

He braced his hands on his knees and groaned, dropping to the ground.

What had he done? He'd let his brother walk out of his life. He couldn't let Helena do that. No, he'd not survive it. He needed her. The montage in his mind of the week he'd just spent with her, of Helena daring him in the art gallery, of her laughing with Leander's friends at the nightclub, or her smiling at the waiter in the small fishing village, and of her looking up at him, playing with that damn necklace that he should have given her himself that Christmas. That Christmas, when she had wanted to give him a present...the one that she'd put in the...

The cubbyhole.

He'd turned back to the house before he'd even realised it and what started as slow steps turned into a jog, driven by an urgency he couldn't name. He shoved through the front door, taking the steps of the staircase two at a time. He came to a stop opposite the painting, imagining a fifteen-year-old Helena outside his room, hearing that she meant nothing to him. *Christós*, his heart buckled in his chest, each beat agony.

With his breath captured in his lungs he lifted the

painting, behind which was a small, dusty shelf on which sat a crumpled box wrapped in faded festive paper.

He reached for it at the same time his phone chimed. Once, twice, and then again. With the present in one hand and his phone in the other, he looked at the message beneath his assistant's name.

Check the news. Right now. Then call me.

Nausea ate at Helena's empty stomach. The moment she had discovered what had happened, she'd called Kate to warn her. And no matter how many times she'd seen the grainy pictures of Kate and Leander passionately kissing, she couldn't stop herself from hoping that somehow the headlines would change.

Twin-Swap Scandal!
Who Married Helena Hadden?
Liassidis Twin Deception!

With shaking hands, she'd scanned an online article written by a blogger who had intended to write an exposé on Californian homes owned by famous Greeks, but had instead stumbled onto an international scandal. He'd identified Leander by spotting him at his home when he'd expected him to be away on his honeymoon and then bribing an usher at a club to photograph Leander with Kate.

Her heart pounded in shock. She'd brought the weight of the world's press down on her two best friends, on Leo; she had ruined *everything*. The guilt was so strong that it blotted out any delight that the two people she had always secretly thought perfect for each other had finally come together.

While reporters had gathered outside the villa, she'd had one harried phone call with her assistant in the UK, and several fraught conversations with the board of Incendia, taking full responsibility for the situation. It was her plan, her choices, that had led the people she cared for most to be caught up in this impossible scandal. All she'd wanted to do was to save Incendia. All she'd wanted to do was to prove that she *could*, that she was worthy to be CEO. That she was *enough*.

But maybe, just maybe, for once there was no fixing it.

It would devastate her to have brought shame to Incendia because of this scandal, but the loss of the money—the issue that would cause them to fail the financial review—that wasn't on her. She had tried to fix it, but it wasn't her fault.

And finally she was beginning to see what Leo had meant.

'It needs to be enough for you, Helena.'

She had tried her hardest. And she had to be okay if that wasn't enough. She *had* to be. Because her mother wasn't going to suddenly be the person Helena wanted her to be. And as much as she could hope that her father would have been proud of her, she had to be proud of herself. And the only way she could still be proud of herself now was to be honest and to face up to the chaos that had happened when people she cared for had tried to help her.

She would put this right as best she could. And there was only one way she could do that. But first she needed to warn Kate what she was going to do.

She picked up the phone and saw missed calls from Leo. She wanted so much to reach out to him, to make sure he was okay. But she couldn't. Not yet. He must be furious at the damage this would do to Liassidis Shipping. Helena could only hope that her plan would deflect as much negativity from him and his company as possible.

She hit call beneath Kate's name on her phone screen.

'Kate?' she asked when the call connected.

'I'm so sorry,' Kate said, her words thick with emotion. 'I've ruined everything.'

'Don't cry,' Helena begged as her best friend's sobs poured out of the phone. 'Please, Kate, don't cry. This is all on me. I begged you to find him when—'

'You didn't.'

'I did. I was so wrapped up in my own problems that I ignored the signs that something was happening between you and sent you to him,' she said, realising the truth as she said it. While Helena had hoped that both Leander and Kate would find the love that they so very much deserved, she'd ignored what was right in front of her in her desperation to make things right at Incendia.

'Nothing was going on before the wedding, I swear. I never meant for anything to happen.'

'I know you didn't,' Helena said, softly and honestly.

'He's coming back to you today, and—'

'I can't be married to Leander, not now. Tell him to stay in California. It's a feeding frenzy here and it's going to get worse before it gets better because I can't do this any more. I'm calling a press conference. There have been so many secrets and lies and so many people hurt that I can't do it any more. I need to tell the truth and—'

'Helena, don't! You'll lose—'

'I have to. I have to put things right. I've hurt so many people,' Helena confessed, shame unspooling in her chest.

'You haven't. You tried so hard to do the right thing and it was for the best of reasons. I'm the one who's screwed everything up.'

'What happened was inevitable. You and Leander are meant to be together,' Helena insisted, thinking of just how perfect they had looked together in the photos. How much in love they'd looked.

Kate's silence on the other end of the phone reached out to Helena's heart. 'It's over.'

'Oh, my love, I'm sorry,' Helena whispered, devastated that they were both feeling the same pain.

'Oh, Helena. Did it happen for you too?'

Helena could barely confess, 'Yes. And it's over too.' She tried so hard to hold back the tears—for herself, for Kate and Leander... They were her family and she had cost them greatly. 'I wasn't enough for him,' she admitted, pain a slow anguish that tightened around her heart with every beat.

'Helena?' Kate's voice was almost a whisper.

'I'm here.'

'Were the Liassidis twins born unfeeling bastards or is it something they cultivated individually as they got older?'

Helena laughed in the way that Kate had always made her laugh, startled, deep and loving. Helena asked Kate about Borneo, promising to come and visit, also promising *not* to kiss any orangutans. And once the laughter had died down, Helena knew that it was time to say goodbye.

'I'm going to make this right,' she swore.

'Are you sure you want to do this?' Kate asked.

'No, but I have to.'

'I wish I could be there to hold your hand through it.'

'I wish you could be too. Have a safe flight to Borneo.'

'I will. Loves ya.'

'Loves ya too,' Helena replied.

After hanging up the phone, she wiped at the trails tears had left on her cheeks, some from heartache and some from laughter. She knew now with absolute certainty that she was doing the right thing.

Leo's pulse raged in time with the whirring of the helicopter blades. The bottom had fallen out of his world the moment he'd seen the first headline. The intense speculation about why the brothers had swapped, who Leander had been caught kissing and who had Helena actually married made his head spin.

His first thought had been Helena. *All* his thoughts had been Helena.

He'd not been able to get her on the phone, so he'd called his assistant and had him send a security team to the villa. But the moment he'd hung up his phone had exploded with phone calls.

He blocked all unknown numbers, and then ignored calls from the Liassidis Shipping board. He could only imagine how terrified they were of stocks and share prices dropping. They probably were, but honestly? Leo couldn't care less. All he could think about was Helena and making sure she was okay.

They landed about ten kilometres from the villa, unable to get closer because of the news helicopters crowding the airspace. The car Leo had arranged waited on the tarmac and as he slid into the dark, cool interior he pulled out his phone and selected a number he hadn't used in years.

He probably should have thought more about this call, but he knew without a shadow of a doubt that once he got his hands on Helena he wasn't going to let her go. His world-renowned focus would be on her, only on her, for the rest of his life. So he needed to do this now.

The phone rang—and a part of him wanted it to keep on ringing. This entire conversation would be easier if he could just leave a message, but he owed it to his brother, owed it to himself, to face up to his responsibility. Only then could he finally move forward. Hopefully, with Helena by his side.

'Naí?'

'It's me,' Leo said.

The pause was so long that Leo had to force himself to relax the grip on his phone before he broke it into a million pieces. There was so much to say. Too much. But if he could at least say the most important thing…

'I'm sorry,' Leo said, his head hung in shame in the

back of the car with no one to see. 'I blamed you for so much. Too much. And I shouldn't have.'

A breath was all Leo heard to let him know that his brother was still on the line. His silence was deserved, Leo had earned that, but at least Leander hadn't ended the call.

'I was…devastated when you chose the money,' Leo admitted. 'I tried to tell myself it was a complete shock to me. That you'd lied to me and that your betrayal was why I was devastated.'

'Leo—'

'Wait, please. I need to say this,' Leo asked, desperate to say his piece. 'The lie was mine, Leander. Because I told myself that I hadn't seen that you were unhappy, that I didn't know you would hate working at Liassidis Shipping, because I was so desperate to cling to our dream. So I pretended that I didn't know, and that I couldn't tell, that it wasn't something you wanted,' he confessed, the dark, furious guilt and anger lessening from telling the truth. 'And I shouldn't have. I'm your brother.'

'*Maláka*, I worked damn hard to make sure you couldn't tell. Give me credit for something,' Leander said, sounding offended.

Against all hope, Leo barked a laugh, a flicker of love spreading throughout his chest.

'You tried to reach out to me and I… I wasn't ready,' Leo tried to explain.

'But you are now? Because of Helena?'

Leo looked up, tilting his head back, hoping that the dampness in his eyes didn't betray him in his voice.

'Is she okay? She told me not to come.' The concern in Leander's voice was as clear when he was talking about Helena as the distance in his tone when speaking to him.

'I'm on my way to make sure she is, right now,' Leo replied with ruthless determination.

There was another long pause.

'Leo, believe me, I appreciate what you're saying, but right now isn't a good time for me. I'm sorry for dragging you into this mess and please, tell Helena that I'm sorry for letting her down.'

Leo gritted his teeth. He knew that his brother's coolness was justified. Five years of complete silence couldn't be undone in one phone call.

You cut her off from everything and everyone she knew.

He had done the same to Leander, his brother, his conscience cried, and guilt opened like a fresh wound across an already battered heart.

'I need to go,' Leander said. 'When I come home we'll talk properly. Okay?'

'Okay. I'd like that,' Leo replied truthfully, thankful for the sliver of hope Leander had created in the darkness.

'So would I,' his brother said before disconnecting the call.

It wasn't the hearts and flowers reunion he might have hoped for, but neither was it an absolute no. It was somewhere to start, and he was okay with that. But it was a very different matter when it came to Helena. As the car took him closer and closer to the villa where he and Helena had arrived only seven days before, Leo grew more and more determined that he would see this through to the end; Helena Hadden was going to be his by the end of the day, no matter what it cost him.

Helena fisted her hand to try and stop her fingers from shaking. The press gathering outside the front of the villa had trebled since the news of her impending state-ment had been released. She risked a glance through the blinds of the windows that looked out at where they were gathered and felt sick.

A line of black-suited men in dark glasses held back the press, preventing them from trying to gain access to the grounds, as one reporter had done just as they'd turned up. Leo had sent them, she knew it.

But she pushed it out of her mind, pushed everything out of her mind, other than what she was about to do. She steeled herself and the nerves went. Because she knew this was the right thing to do. And she knew that, no matter what the outcome was, she would have done everything in her power to protect those she loved. And that was enough for her. It might not be everything she'd ever wanted, but she was at peace with it.

He had seen her. Leo had. He had recognised her as good at what she did. Celebrated that with her. But he'd been right. No one could give her what she needed. Not him. Not her parents. She had to give that to herself. She had to be enough for *herself.*

Helena smoothed down the dress she had chosen to wear—a simple cornflower-blue muslin V-neck. Her hair, blonde and down, made her feel pretty, feminine and *her*. That was how she wanted to meet the press.

She opened the front door and walked on the grey stone slabs towards the gate to the villa, where one of Leo's bodyguards stood to attention, hands clasped in front of him.

'Ma'am.'

She nodded and he pulled open the gate, and the sudden cry of voices and stuttered flashbulbs hit her like a meteor shower. Drawing on an inner strength she didn't know she had, she walked out into the villa's courtyard, where Leo's other men were holding the press at bay. She waited until the press had calmed themselves, until the camera flashes slowed and the questions halted.

'I'm going to make a statement which will cover as much as possible at this time,' she explained. 'And if you have questions, I will try to answer them honestly.'

A few flashes went off, but predominantly the paparazzi remained quiet.

'Six months ago, I was made CEO of a charity I not only believe in, but personally benefitted from after the sudden death of my father when I was sixteen years old. Incendia raises not only money but awareness, grief support, therapy and research into rare cardiac diseases that are of no financial interest to big pharmaceutical companies. In short, it's a godsend to those who need to rely on it,' she said, a sad smile coming to her lips.

She took a breath. 'Shortly after taking up the position, I discovered that an employee had stolen nearly one hundred million pounds from the charity and disappeared.' She pushed on through the gasp of shock.

'The previous CEO had failed to renew the business insurance and the charity will likely fail the financial review in December.

'But what does all this have to do with the Liassidis brothers?' she asked rhetorically.

She smiled when one reporter cried out, 'Yes!' much to the amusement of many present.

'My father left me an inheritance. An inheritance that will mature when I am either twenty-eight years old or when I marry. I had hoped to use that inheritance to cover the gap in Incendia's finances. I know that this was wrong, but I was desperate for Incendia to keep on doing the good work that it does,' she said truthfully, feeling the damp heat of tears against the backs of her eyes.

'Leander Liassidis offered to loan me the money, but… I *have* the money…or would have it in two years' time, but for an arbitrary bit of wording that would have taken too long to challenge legally. So we decided to marry.

'Please. Let me explain. I love Leander. Truly. But only like a brother. And while no one, not even he, thought he'd ever settle down, he *did* meet someone. A very special someone, whom I love dearly. But that story is theirs to tell.

'When Leander left, Leo Liassidis stepped in so that I wouldn't be humiliated in front of the world on my wedding day. He too wanted nothing more than to help me. And words will never express how much that meant to me,' she said, her throat becoming thick with emotion.

'I assure you that the marriage certificate will never

be submitted to the registrar's office and, as such, the ceremony from that day is not legally binding. Leander Liassidis and I are not married.

'I want to make it *very* clear that the Liassidis brothers did nothing but try to help a family friend in trouble. They are two of the most honourable men I have ever met and I am lucky to have them in my life.'

Was lucky, she mentally clarified, the thought striking her silent.

'Are there any questions?' she asked.

'Did he sign his own name, Helena?'

She frowned into the crowed, unsure where the question came from and unable to see from the lights that had been set up to point at her.

'I don't know,' she said honestly. 'I signed first so I didn't see the signature.'

'Was the priest involved?' another faceless questioner asked.

'Absolutely not. Again, to make this clear—this entire mess was of my making. When Leander and I decided to marry, we couldn't have imagined the press interest in the relationship, and from there things spiralled out of control. Please know that I am *solely* responsible for this and the Liassidis brothers have done nothing that I didn't ask them to do first.'

'So you have no feelings—no romantic feelings—for Leander Liassidis?' someone asked, the voice slightly drowned out by other questions, but oddly familiar.

'No,' she confirmed. 'Absolutely not. Nothing has or ever will happen between us in that way.'

'But what about Leo Liassidis?' the same person

asked, slowly pushing their way through the throng. Helena's pulse began to pound in her chest, goosebumps rising across the delicate skin on her forearms and the back of her neck.

'Excuse me?' she asked, hesitating for the first time since stepping out into the throng of reporters.

'Do you have any romantic feelings for *him*?' the person prompted again, this time the crowd parting enough for Helena to see Leo Liassidis standing before her—in the middle of a sea of reporters ready to cast the news around the world.

'What are you...?'

Didn't he realise that she was trying to extricate him from this mess? That she was trying to protect him? He was throwing away everything he had for her when all she could do was ruin him.

'Do you,' Leo asked, his eyes locked onto hers, hope and more filling her with every passing second, 'have feelings for me?'

A gasp of shock rippled through the press watching with unabashed interest.

'I...'

'Because I have it on good authority,' he said, to the general laughter of the men and women around him, 'that he has feelings for you. Very strong feelings. In fact,' he said, all cocky arrogance and handsomeness, just like he used to have before the separation with his brother had made him hard, 'I'm pretty sure he's in love with you.'

Her heart soared, breaking through the agony of the

last twelve hours. Tears came to her eyes and a sob filled her chest, even as her lips pulled into a shocked smile.

'If you're only *pretty sure…*' she replied with teasing hesitation.

'I love you,' he called out loudly, without question and without any of the cocky arrogance from before. The moment was caught by a billion flashbulbs exploding as they stared at each other across the courtyard.

A feeling of effervescent completeness filled her. It was a high that she would never come down from. He was everything she had always wanted. There had never been anyone else for her, no one had made her feel as wanted, as cherished, as *loved.*

He loved her. He loved her even though she could ruin Liassidis Shipping with the bad press that would surely follow this scandal, and he was smiling at her as if he didn't care.

'I love everything about you,' he confessed. 'I love how much you care, I love how hard you try, and I love how much you inspire me and others to be better than ourselves. You are funny, and sexy and smart and I want to marry you. Again. Under my own name this time,' he said to the laughter of the press. 'I've known you for many, many years, but,' he said, taking something out of his pocket and holding it up, '"*sometimes you have to go it alone to know your own worth*",' he quoted.

Helena shivered—it was the watch, the silly watch she'd bought him all those Christmases ago. The battery must have died long ago, but the inscription she'd asked to be put on the back of the watch probably still clear as day. It was an inscription that had been—at the time—about him and Leander, but somehow was even more fitting for *them*.

'We've both done it alone and we know how strong we are, so now let's find out how unbeatable we are together?'

Leo's breath was locked in his chest.

He could see the tears glistening in her eyes, feel the pounding of her heart in time with his own. He'd meant every word he'd said and he genuinely didn't care if Liassidis Shipping disappeared tomorrow, as long as he was by Helena's side. In seven days she had become his world. She was the light, the sky, the ground beneath his feet, the sun, moon and stars above; she was the only person he would ever need in his life.

Her smile wobbled as she took a tentative step towards him. It was all he needed as he closed the distance between them in a heartbeat, taking her into his arms with a kiss that sent off another thousand sparks. A kiss that would appear on headlines around the world for years to come. A kiss that had many names, but the only one of real importance was theirs: true love's kiss.

'I love you,' Helena pressed against his lips. 'I've always loved you,' she said again.

'I'm sorry it took me so long to get here,' he said, thinking of how long it had taken him to realise how much he lived for her. 'You are the most precious thing in the world to me and I'll not let a single day pass without letting you know that,' he promised.

'Okay,' she said, looking up at him with a love so strong and so sure he could barely believe it.

'Okay?' he asked, unsure what she was agreeing to.

'I'll marry you,' she said. *'Again.'* And through the re-sounding cheers of celebration from the reporters around them, for the first time in years Leo felt the missing part of his heart return and completeness filled him as he gave Helena his heart, unchecked and untamed.

He kissed her again then, the first of many that would litter their lives like stars in the night sky. Theirs was a happiness proclaimed to the world as true love, from that moment until their very last breaths.

EPILOGUE

Two years later...

LEO LOOKED AT himself in the mirror, fixing his cuff-links, assessing his appearance with a more critical eye than usual. He took in the dark trousers, the morning coat, the waistcoat.

'Tell me again that I'm doing the right thing.'

'You are doing what you *need* to.'

'Am I?'

'Leo, if you want me to talk you out of this, I can,' his brother offered, holding his gaze in the reflection of the mirror.

'Would you?'

'No. Not really. Kate would kill me if I tried to talk you out of this now.'

Leo barked out a laugh. Leander was absolutely right and, while he'd never tell a soul, secretly, he was slightly terrified of his sister-in-law.

'This is what Helena wanted, and I will do whatever it takes to make her happy,' Leo told himself.

Leander slapped him on the back. 'That's the spirit.'

He'd wanted a small ceremony, something quiet and

intimate. Helena had done much in the last few years to bring him out of his shell, but Leo was still more inclined to prefer smaller gatherings. But he'd do anything for his future wife, the least of which was having the wedding of her dreams.

Which was why they were in an English Tudor mansion and he was about to put on, of all things, a top hat.

An actual top hat.

'Apparently, she said it made you look handsome,' Leander said, eyeing the damn thing with as much suspicion as Leo felt.

'I don't need a hat to make me look handsome,' Leo replied coolly.

'You keep telling yourself that, brother,' Leander said, with another pat on his shoulder.

'I don't know what you're laughing about. You have to wear one too.'

Leander's face was a picture. A snapshot of a mixture of fear and horror.

'No,' he said, shaking his head, his hand slashing through the air definitively. 'I love you. I do. But not that much.'

Leo couldn't help it. He threw his head back and laughed.

'I'm pretty sure that Kate would kill you if you ruined Helena's wedding,' Leo pointed out when he regained a little of his composure.

Leander glared at the box in the corner of the room, the muscle in his jaw clenching. 'The things we do for these women we love,' he growled and stalked over to the box, opening it and retrieving his own top hat. He practically snarled at the thing.

It had been nearly two years since Leo and Leander had reunited. The phone call Leo had made just before Helena's press conference had been the start of the road that brought them back together.

That day had changed Leo's life irrevocably. The darkness that had shrouded his life, the heavy weight that he'd tried to pretend had been work and pressure, had lifted. Because he'd finally realised what he needed and wanted from his life, and it had nothing to do with Liassidis Shipping.

Love. Peace. Contentment. *Family.*

When Leander had returned from California they had met and talked long into the night. Both had felt responsible for the separation in their own way, and perhaps it had been partly necessary. They had grown up as two halves of a whole, and had needed to find themselves as individuals as much as twins. But, having done that, they could now appreciate the differences between them as much as the similarities. And their relationship now was based on that understanding and a thousand times stronger for it. The pieces of his life's puzzle had come together to form a picture he'd always wanted.

But it had been complete the moment that Helena agreed to be his wife.

It hadn't been easy—those first few months after the discovery that Leander had been in California and that Leo had been pretending to be him in Greece had caused a lot of anger in the press. Liassidis Shipping stocks and shares had taken a sharp fall and it had been a nail-biting year, watching them slowly come back up as everyone realised that his and Helena's feelings were real. That theirs was the true love story they'd been looking for after all.

Interestingly, Helena's announcement had caused a spike in attention for Incendia, her raw honesty and natural passion as she had spoken about the charity catching the world's imagination.

Donations had started to pour in for the charity from around the globe and within two months they had reached enough to cover a large portion of the money stolen—enough to survive the financial review. Gregory had been found and charged with fraud and financial theft and a slew of other smaller offences.

The trial was due to begin at the end of the following month, the wheels of justice turning painfully slowly. But at least they were turning. Helena was convinced of a positive outcome and had been happy to recover even just half of what had been stolen, the remaining assets lost somewhere in the Caymans was as good a guess as any.

Leander cleared his throat from where he held the door open with one hand, and chucked the top hat at him with the other. Leo caught the brim and, with a huge amount of trepidation, secured it on his head.

'It's showtime,' his brother announced.

Leo stopped at the threshold. 'Thank you,' he said to Leander sincerely.

Leander nodded, for once casting aside the playful persona. He knew how much this meant to Leo, knew that he wanted to honour that for his brother.

'It wouldn't have been the same without you,' Leo said.

'No party ever is, Leo!' he replied, the smile broadening on features that matched his own.

And Leo agreed. Nothing had been right without his brother in his life, but now that he was back it was just as perfect as he remembered from his childhood. That sense of lack, of loss, of something missing, had been found. Not just with his brother but with the woman he was about to marry. If Leander had been a missing piece, Helena had been his missing heart. And he couldn't wait to declare to the world that she was his, to love, to honour, to protect, to worship and to always, *always*, put first.

Leo had to admit that the Tudor mansion in the Suffolk countryside was spectacular. The thick white stone walls had stood strong against the march of time, and the casement windows punctuating the unique architecture were nothing short of eye-catching. Inside, dark wood panels lined some rooms, while raw stone added rustic features to an already impressive historic building. Four-poster beds welcomed each guest, while open fireplaces and richly coloured carpets added comfort to a luxury that was nothing short of exquisite.

As Leander led him through to the chapel nestled in the gardens where the ceremony would take place he began to feel his pulse picking up. Not for himself, not for the commitment he was about to make to the woman he loved beyond question. But for her. He wanted, needed, this to be perfect for her. With absolutely no doubt about him or his intentions.

Which was why, the night before last, he'd given her a gift—not a wedding gift, no. He had other ideas for that. But as they'd sat in the London apartment where they spent half the year, sharing a glass of wine after dinner, he'd passed across the document he'd asked his lawyers to draw up.

'What's this?' she'd asked. 'You've already given me my birthday present,' she said, smiling saucily.

'Open it and see.'

And he'd watched her read through the document, surprise, delight and love glittering in the sheen that filled her gaze.

'It's not supposed to make you sad, *agápi mou*,' he'd insisted.

It was a document releasing her father's inheritance. The thirty percent shares in Liassidis Shipping. Helena had wanted to marry as soon as they could, but Leo had insisted on waiting until after her twenty-eighth birthday, because whether she needed it or not, *he* did. Because when he married her, he wanted to be the *only* thing on her mind that day.

She'd shaken her head, the smile on her lips purely happy. 'I'm not sad, my love. Not at all. Just happy. Just absolutely, ridiculously happy. Thank you. So much. This means the world,' she'd said before she'd kissed him with one of those drugging kisses that made him lose all sense and reason, and utterly unashamed that he'd not even been able to wait to get her to the bedroom. He'd pulled her across his lap and they'd made love long into the night.

And so it was for the final time that Leo found himself standing at the top of an aisle, waiting for Helena to walk to him.

'Nervous?' Leander asked.

'Not a single bit,' he said truthfully.

'I think we should swap places,' Leander teased. 'Do you think they'd notice?'

'Yes,' Leo replied without a doubt. Because Helena and Kate had *always* noticed—the only two women, aside from their mother, to have ever been able to tell them apart. It was as if he and Leander had always been known, always been loved by the women who had captured their hearts.

Right then, the doors opened and Leo lost his breath.

If Helena had looked amazing two years ago, it was nothing compared to how she looked that day. Dressed in cream silk that clung lovingly to her chest and flared out carefully over the rounded curve of her stomach, she rested the bouquet of pink and white peonies gently on her seven-month baby bump.

A wave of emotion like he'd never felt before swept over Leo. The adoration he felt for her, the worship he wanted to lay at her feet. She was a miracle and he the luckiest man alive.

Kate stepped up beside Helena, having agreed to Helena's request for her to walk her down the aisle, and Leo barely felt Leander stiffen beside him, because all of his renowned focus was entirely on Helena. The true love of his life.

He barely heard the words the priest said that day. And when they signed the register, with Kate and Leander as their witnesses, they all shared a small smile at the memory of how they'd all come together.

But, in truth, Leo didn't need a piece of paper to declare them joined. He had given his heart away years before and nothing would take that away. And this time, when the priest asked if he would take Helena to be his wife, his love, his heart…there was nothing temporary about his answer.

He meant it with his entire soul.

'I do.'

* * * * *

Did you fall head over heels for
Greek's Temporary "I Do"?
Then you're sure to adore the first installment in
The Greek Groom Swap duet

The Forbidden Greek
by Michelle Smart!

And don't miss out on these other Pippa Roscoe stories:

The Wife the Spaniard Never Forgot
Expecting Her Enemy's Heir
His Jet-Set Nights with the Innocent
In Bed with Her Billionaire Bodyguard
Twin Consequences of That Night

Available now!